LEMARTES

SPACE MARINE
LEGENDS

LEMARTES

DAVID ANNANDALE

BLACK LIBRARY

For my parents, Eric and Eleanor Annandale. For everything.

A BLACK LIBRARY PUBLICATION

Lemartes first published in 2015.
This edition published in Great Britain in 2017 by
Black Library,
Games Workshop Ltd.,
Willow Road,
Nottingham, NG7 2WS, UK.

10 9 8 7 6 5 4 3 2 1

Produced by Games Workshop in Nottingham.
Cover illustration by Neil Roberts.

See Black Library on the internet at

blacklibrary.com

Find out more about Games Workshop
and the world of Warhammer 40,000 at

games-workshop.com

Printed and bound in China

It is the 41st millennium. For more than a hundred centuries the Emperor has sat immobile on the Golden Throne of Earth. He is the master of mankind by the will of the gods, and master of a million worlds by the might of his inexhaustible armies. He is a rotting carcass writhing invisibly with power from the Dark Age of Technology. He is the Carrion Lord of the Imperium for whom a thousand souls are sacrificed every day, so that he may never truly die.

Yet even in his deathless state, the Emperor continues his eternal vigilance. Mighty battlefleets cross the daemon infested miasma of the warp, the only route between distant stars, their way lit by the Astronomican, the psychic manifestation of the Emperor's will. Vast armies give battle in His name on uncounted worlds. Greatest amongst his soldiers are the Adeptus Astartes, the Space Marines, bioengineered super-warriors. Their comrades in arms are legion: the Astra Militarum and countless planetary defence forces, the ever-vigilant Inquisition and the tech-priests of the Adeptus Mechanicus to name only a few. But for all their multitudes, they are barely enough to hold off the ever-present threat from aliens, heretics, mutants – and worse.

To be a man in such times is to be one amongst untold billions. It is to live in the cruellest and most bloody regime imaginable. These are the tales of those times. Forget the power of technology and science, for so much has been forgotten, never to be re-learned. Forget the promise of progress and understanding, for in the grim dark future there is only war. There is no peace amongst the stars, only an eternity of carnage and slaughter, and the laughter of thirsting gods.

CHAPTER ONE

Evangelical

An ocean in storm: blood to infinite depths, rage the sum of all tempests and waves breaking into crimson foam as they crash against the obsidian sky. A presence approaching. The thing of rage and blood. Born of the storm, shaper of the ocean. A terrible rising. The bringer of the roar, endless and final, a roar of reason's death and of fury's dominion. The destroyer still in the shadow of the sky, concealed by the waves, but coming in wrath. Inexorable. Inevitable.

The need for clarity.
The dread of revelation.
The retaliation of my own rage.
A war of storms.

* * *

Baldwin Morrov knew when the prayers on Phleg-ethon stopped. He felt it– the hard snap of spiritual abandonment. The cord that had linked him from this tomb of darkness and bloodshed to the hope of rescue and light had thinned, frayed, and now was gone. He even knew who had been the last to turn away: his children. They were called Alayna and Bernd, but he had lost their names some time ago. Even their faces were darkening blurs in the shards that remained of his identity. But that any-thing remained was due to their prayers.

Morrov was not a psyker, yet some agency had per-mitted him to feel the psychic ripples of the prayers. In the first days of his entombment, the hope had sustained his rational being. The Morrov of the early days of the ordeal had believed the hand of the Emperor was behind the miracle.

But when the rescue did not come, and the prayers began to fall away, the loss of hope was worse than if it had never been present. In the dying moments of Morrov's self, he had known the Emperor was not blessing him. And then had come the blasphemous thought that something else might be at work. That terror had marked his last coherent thought.

And now the final connection was broken. He howled. He crawled forward in the dark. His work uniform was rags, and the stones dug into his flesh. His hands, thick with scar tissue and bleed-ing from fresh cuts, touched something that moved. It screamed and attacked him. Hands squeezed his throat. He fought back and felt his broken nails sink into softness. He dug deeper. The other's screams turned desperate. The hands released his throat. Morrov breathed and snarled. He pushed and tore and gouged until the screams and the struggling and the movement stopped.

But the darkness did not stop. Morrov kept growling as if to keep the suffocating silence at bay.

He did not know that he had just killed his friend Teodor Weiss. But then, Weiss had forgotten his own name some time ago. Weiss, like Morrov, had become a bundle of fearful, raging instincts, moving and fighting in darkness.

And eating.

Morrov began to feast.

There was so much gone from the ruin of Baldwin Morrov. He did not know where he was, or how he had come to be there. He did not remember being a miner. He did not know that he was in one of the largest of the thousands of small moons that orbited Phlegethon in a thick cloud. Some were a few metres in size. Others were hundreds of kilometres in diameter. Rich in ore, this particular moonlet's interior had become the site of a gigantic mining operation. Atmosphere generators permitted work unfettered by void suits. Enough miners to populate a small city had worked the veins for over a century.

But then, the catastrophe. Morrov no longer had a memory of the time before the cataclysm, but what was left of his mind did retain an impression of the coming of night, so deep were the wounds. Even in the first days of darkness, when the trapped souls were still cooperating, still hoping, and still thinking, Morrov had not learned the cause of his entombment. He did not know that he was a victim of chance and gravity. The density of Phlegethon's moon swarm was such that collisions were inevitable. The mining asteroid had been struck by another chunk of rock, one much smaller, but large enough that the blast had destroyed all surface installations and collapsed the access to the mines.

Power had failed. Light had died. Enough of the moon had been excavated over the decades that its volume contained sufficient breathable atmosphere for months. But there was only enough food for weeks. As the days had passed and rescue had not come, cooperation had given way to competition for the diminishing resources. And competition had given way to war.

Light was the edge. Light was the key to finding stores and spotting those who would take them. Portable lamps became more precious than the food itself. They became targets. Once the battles began in earnest, it was only a matter of days before night came to the tunnels, never to leave.

The war had taken Morrov apart. It had broken him down to the most desperate core. Existence had become nothing but the struggle in the void, and when there was not struggle, there was the silence that waited beyond death. And running through all those days of torment was the rage.

The rage against enemies. Against fate. Against the dark. Against the rescuers who would not come.

And when he had still been capable of speech, and of understanding it, Morrow had heard blasphemous rage against the Emperor Himself.

Morrow had uttered no such heresy. There had been that cord of hope. He had known there were prayers. They had sustained him, given him strength to endure. When they had begun to die away, they had given him the strength of desperation.

And now, snap. The hope that he no longer comprehended but needed beyond all measure vanished.

The rage took him. The rage that had built up inside the stone prison. The rage of thousands and thousands of humans tearing each other apart in despair. The rage of final betrayal. A concentrated essence. A summation.

The conclusion of the first step of a very great work.

Morrow shrieked in the silence. He crawled through blood and over bones. He clawed at stone. When he encountered a rising slope of fallen rock, he hurled himself against the barrier. He battered his bones and flesh against the seal of his tomb. His ragged lungs took a deep breath of foul air. He screamed the full enormity of his mindless rage and perfect hate. The god he had worshipped did not hear him.

But another did.

Stones shifted.

Phlegethon's days of miracles began.

* * *

Lina Elsener waited in the medicae centre for the shuttle to deliver the survivor. The centre was located near the top of the apex spire of Hive Profundis and close to the tower's landing pad.

'Why are they bringing him here?' Mirus Thulin asked. 'He's a serf.'

'He's a miracle,' Elsener told him, 'and miracles must be honoured.' She wasn't really joking. She understood the political calculations of the decision. The tens of thousands of miners who had died in the disaster had had enough connections that a significant portion of the hive's population had been affected to at least some degree. When the last attempts to reach the entombed had been abandoned, and all hope finally lost, the unrest had continued. The smooth functioning of other orbital operations had been compromised. The expense involved in crushing resistance and forcing reluctant serfs back to work was considerable. A display of generosity towards the sole survivor made sound economic sense.

But the fact of the matter was that the patient Elsener was going to receive *was* a miracle. He should not be alive. The crew that had picked him up had voxed that he was in a vegetative state, and Elsener thought it likely that he would never recover. But he was alive. Not only that, he had somehow managed to break through the rubble to a pocket near the surface where there had been a functioning beacon. Which he had activated.

That, at least, was what had been reported. Elsener

had her doubts. If he was in a coma, how had he triggered the beacon? She wasn't even sure it was a beacon that had summoned the rescue team. She had known about the call before it had been announced. Everyone had. That was part of the miracle. The God-Emperor had directed the attention of all Phlegethon to the moon at that vital moment. That was the explanation.

Surely it was. Nothing else made sense.

But the doubts were there. She should have been ecstatic to be among the first to see this wonder, and to be the chirurgeon responsible for his care. Instead, tension was twisting her gut. When she swallowed, she tasted bile.

She glanced at Thulin. If her assistant was worried, he didn't show it. He seemed much more offended by the impropriety of a mining serf receiving the treatment reserved for the nobility of Profundis.

'He shouldn't be here,' Thulin insisted.

'It is the governor's will,' Elsener said. She was about to add, 'And the Emperor's.' The tension choked off her words. Instead, she walked to the entrance of the medicae centre. She looked down the hall adorned by the ruling family's banners. Beyond the closed iron doors at the end, she heard the roar of the approaching shuttle's retro-engines. Her charge was almost here.

She drummed her fingers against the doorway. The tension was resolving itself into a war between fear and anger. She didn't know why.

The doors banged open. Elsener's eyes widened. Lord Governor Uhlen entered, ahead of a cluster of his household servants bearing the stretcher on which lay the miracle. *Of course,* Elsener thought. *The governor must be known to have greeted the survivor and escorted him to care. Of course.*

She had to fight to keep her face from twisting into a snarl. In the next second, as she became aware of the struggle, her skin pricked with fear.

Elsener stepped to the side of the door, folded her arms in her chirurgeon's robes, and bowed her head in greeting to the governor. Uhlen's nod was curt. He walked to the nearest operating table. His servants transferred the miner from the stretcher and withdrew.

'Well?' Uhlen asked as Elsener approached. His thin lips were compressed. A vein was throbbing on his neck. 'Can you do anything with him?'

'I will need to examine him first,' she answered, thinking she was doing very well to remain civil.

'Do your work well, chirurgeon,' Uhlen said. 'If he dies, he does more harm than if he'd never emerged.'

'I will do what is possible to be done.' Her first sight of the miner was not encouraging. Even though he had been cleaned by the shuttle crew, he was a bloody mass of wounds and contusions. His face was so damaged it was doubtful anyone would be able to identify him. Tracking down who he was would be time-consuming. At least that was none of her concern.

She reached out to take his pulse. Her fingers touched his arm. It snapped up and he grabbed her by the wrist. When she tried to pull away, he sat up. His eyes opened. For a moment, they were an unfocused, cloudy green, staring blankly at the opposite wall.

Then a murderous scarlet spread out from his pupils, filled the irises, and then the whites. His eyes were a uniform red, but they were not blind or unfocused now. They glinted with passion and knowledge. He looked first straight ahead at the governor, and then turned his head to face Elsener. She saw the true fire in his gaze. She felt the wrath of thousands upon thousands of raging souls strike her.

In the corners of her vision, blood appeared. It was running down the walls and across the floor of the medicae centre. It poured from the ceiling. It sprang from every surface in the hall.

It ran in tears down her face, but there was no grief. Nor was there fear. She did not hold back her snarl now.

'What is there but rage?' asked the Prophet of Blood.

Beyond the huge sprawl of Hive Profundis were the great prairies of Phlegethon's northern continent. Millennia of polluted atmosphere, diminished sunlight and overwork of the land were pushing what had been the most fertile region on the planet towards desertification. Millions of hectares had become mud fields. Wind storms blew topsoil into the sky, leaving dead earth behind. But many of the great farms were still active. The hive must be fed, and ways were found. The time would come when even the most desperate measures would not be enough. But that time had not come yet.

On the edges of the giant concerns were a few smaller holdings, fragments owned by the last representatives of once-great families. They had been nobles. Now they were one or two generations away from beggars. Albrecht Cawler knew enough of his family history to know that his ancestors had been wealthy. But that was so many centuries in the past, the knowledge had no emotional resonance for him. What mattered was the present, and the present was the need to raise enough grain to keep the struggle going another year.

Cawler was walking back from his field towards his sagging farmhouse when he heard thunder. He glanced up. The night sky, lit by the glow of the hive, was a uniform black and amber. There were no storm clouds.

The thunder continued. The rumble grew louder. It seemed to be coming from behind him. He turned around.

Cawler's farm ended at a baked clay plain that ran straight to the hundred-metre-high walls of Hive Profundis. The hive rose from the plain with the sudden, vertical thrust of a monstrous horn jutting from the earth. Level upon level, spire upon spire, it was a tapering cone of agglomerated architecture that towered past the clouds. A hundred million people lived there, their competing faith, duty and need and ambitions, hatreds and desires crawling over one another in an unending battle whose goals ranged from the luxury and prestige of the highest peaks to simple survival in the underhive depths.

The thunder came from the hive. It built and built until the rumbles became hammer blows against a drum the size of the world. Cawler covered his ears. Terror pushed him to his knees. The greatest crash of all came, and it seemed to Cawler that the entire hive shook. Its lights flickered, then flared red. A million eyes glared out of the night.

The thunder faded, and gave way to a new sound. It was a roar. It began as distant waves on a rocky shore. The waves came closer, and there was no receding before the next crash. Closer. The roar was hungry. Cawler began to pray.

The wave burst from the gates of Hive Profundis. Cawler's prayer faltered. He stared at a rushing mob of hundreds, of thousands, of hundreds of thousands, and still more. The gates were wide, the flow was unending, and the roar came from the throats of uncountable monsters. Caught in the grip of a rage that knew neither mercy, nor obstacle, nor surcease, the citizens of Profundis raced over the land.

Cawler screamed at the most terrible sight he had ever witnessed.

But then the wave reached him.

* * *

The sky above the colony was dark with smoke. The ruins were shrouded with it. Not a single building still stood. Khevrak strode over the wreckage. His neuroglottis filtered the component elements of the smoke. It sorted the burning wood from the smouldering plasteel, the promethium from the human flesh. There was a lot of flesh. The colonists of Algidus lay in huge pyres, hills of bodies many metres high, towering over the remnants of their homes. Khevrak passed between two of the mounds. He walked through a valley of death that he had called into being. The guttering flames reflected off the brass and black of his power armour. The armour was his identity. He was the darkness that came with night, and he was the unforgiving strength of metal. The brass of his helmet was the echo of fire and blood, the wrath of the Blood God forged into a skull of war. On his left shoulder plate was a different sort of skull. Horned, elongated, the badge was the symbol for the carnage that surrounded Khevrak. It was death, and it was inhuman. So was every action undertaken by Khevrak's warband.

In this moment, as he walked, all Khevrak could see and hear and taste was devastation. This was good work. But it was not sufficient. How could it be, when there was an entire galaxy to feed to the Blood God? Already, the hunger for death, driven by unending anger, was growing again. There were moments of satisfaction, in the heat of battle, in the highest peaks of slaughter, when the world was drenched in vitae and it seemed that life itself would finally drown in its own essence. Those were the moments when Khevrak believed his worship took on its purest, most potent form. He felt on the verge of transformation, then, touching the apotheosis that would be the ultimate expression of what it meant to be one of the Blood Disciples.

But the slaughter was always finite. It always ended. The Blood Disciples were constrained in their offerings by the limits of their military capability. Transcendence remained out of reach.

Khevrak reached the centre of the colony. This was where the chapel had been. The greatest massacre had taken place here, but so many of the bodies had become ash that the mounds were lower than elsewhere. The only trace of the chapel that remained was the blackened stones of its foundations. They were the bones of slain belief. At the heart of the wreckage, the Dark Apostle knelt.

Khevrak stopped outside the perimeter of the defiled chapel and waited. He would not disturb Dhassaran at his devotions. Around the Apostle, corpses lay in jagged angles, spines and limbs shattered into runic symbols. A nimbus of energy crackled over Dhassaran. It was the colour of rust and violence. It twisted the air. It dragged claws over space. Even outside the area of the ritual, Khevrak could feel a tug. The aura was the trace of pure hunger, an abstraction seeking to reify itself. It was the sign of Dhassaran finding another step along the path towards the Blood Disciples' destiny.

There was a flash, the shriek of reality sliced with an axe, and the nimbus vanished. Dhassaran rose. He turned and walked out of the circle of corpses towards Khevrak. The robe he wore over his armour smoked. Prayer scrolls of human flesh were curled, their edges burned. Dhassaran had begun the ceremony as the chapel burned down around him. There were new scorch marks on his face, adding to the topography of scarred and burned tissue. Deep in his skull, his eyes burned more brightly than the colony had at the height of the conflagration. His lips were pulled back in an eager, ecstatic snarl.

'You have seen something,' Khevrak said.

'I have, brother-captain. And I have news. The time of our transcendence approaches.'

'We have always believed that.'

'Yes, but now I know where.' Dhassaran spread his arms wide and tilted his head back, welcoming the atrocities to come. 'The Prophet of Blood is reborn,' he said.

Joy was a thing of blades and ragged wounds. Khevrak experienced joy now. 'You're sure?' he asked.

Dhassaran nodded once. 'I experienced his return in my vision. He has come. And so, at last, has our transcendence. And redemption.'

Redemption. It was a word that passed the lips of very few who were sworn to Chaos. 'Redemption,' Khevrak said, tasting the syllables, exploring their razored edges. The chance had come for the Blood Disciples to atone for the crime that had given them birth. Before the great conversion, before the end of delusion, they had been the Emperor's Wolves. In the name of the false god, they had killed the Prophet of Blood. That act had been their last in the service of the Imperium. From that moment onward, they had been disciples to Khorne. But they had silenced the voice that spoke of the way forwards.

At last, the voice had returned.

'Redemption,' Dhassaran repeated. 'He waits for us on Phlegethon.'

The storm. The ocean. The blood. The shadow moving closer. A great blow descending.

Then Corbulo stands before me. He watches me without speaking. I step out of my stasis chamber. 'Ask me,' I say.

'What do you see?'

The blur. Sanguinary priest and primarch. Overlap of images, their features identical. Phantom wings. The need to fight, to save Sanguinius this time, this now. Kill the traitor Horus.

No. I know who is present. I will myself to see him. Cracks of black and flickers of red withdraw to the edges of my vision. I hold them there. I hold back the tide.

The tide that never ebbs.

'I see you, Brother Corbulo.' Every word a bloodied victory. A bitter irony. I am a Chaplain. Before the Rage, words were in my arsenal. Their shaping was a duty. Words to inspire. Words to condemn. Words to blast the souls of the enemy. But now every rational syllable is carved from the cliff face of rage. The rage of a madman. I am that madman. I am sane only as long as I know that I am mad. The madness will drown me if I ever think myself sane.

'What else do you see?'

The banners of victories surrounding us, hanging in the still air. I know what every battle was, though I do not always remember them. But Corbulo asks if I know where I am. 'The chamber,' I tell him. 'My crypt.' My needed prison. Deep in Mount Seraph. Beneath the cells that hold my brothers of the Death Company. I can hear their shouts through the rock. But I do not know if those sounds are real.

My hands are closed into fists. They grip reality. It is slippery.

Corbulo says, 'The Death Company is needed, Chaplain Lemartes.'

'Rage to combat rage,' I say.

He looks at me sharply. 'Why do you say that?'

'Am I wrong?'

'No.' He pauses. 'The precise nature of the crisis is as yet unclear.'

'Clear enough to wake me.' I am the sleeping monster. I have no consciousness except for war and its preparation.

'Yes,' says Corbulo. 'Phlegethon, in the Caïna sector, has been struck with what appears to be a plague of wrath. The Mordian Iron Guard has intervened.

They have been unable to restore order or stem the spread of the infection.'

'A plague of wrath,' I repeat. Fury taking the form of a disease. Corbulo watches as I consider the parallels. Whatever is happening on Phlegethon is not the Black Rage. There is a link, though. I do not believe in a coincidence of symptoms.

The vision. The roaring shadow. A thing of anger and strength. Grasping.

Squeeze of fists. Willed clarity. This vision is important. There is a link between Phlegethon and my madness.

Corbulo says, 'You don't appear surprised.'

'I am not.'

'Why did you say, "Rage to combat rage"? How could you know?'

'A vision.'

'From the Heresy?'

'Not of that fall. Nor of mine.' The slippages of time, of place, the confusion of the real. Of late, I have walked again on Hadriath XI. I have Corbulo to thank for a new layer of delusion. We both know this. He regrets the added martyrdom. He will not, though, desist in his research. I would not wish him to. I give my strength to the Chapter, to Sanguinius. And my soul. And my madness.

I describe the vision to Corbulo. It slips over the real. *Storm. Blood. Shadow.* The vault of the chamber rises into limbo. Stone becomes insubstantial. The flagstones beneath my boots sink beneath waves. I feel the wind. It reeks of death. It cries with violence. The blood rises past my waist, to my neck.

Submerging.

No.

Push it away.

Stone beneath me. The sacred hardness of Baal around me. The Sanguinary High Priest watching and listening.

'That is no memory,' Corbulo says. He is holding a data-slate, taking notes. He did not have it when I began speaking. Reality moved on while I was in the storm. 'But you have not mentioned it before.'

'It is new.'

'Since last we spoke?'

'Yes.' The implications are clear to both of us.

'There are no dreams in stasis,' Corbulo says.

'I know.'

'They do not happen,' he insists, as if I have contradicted him.

'This was no dream.'

He muses. 'Perhaps, during the transition out of stasis...'

I turn from him and walk to a recess in the far corner of the chamber. This is my cell. Here are my weapons. Here is my helmet. 'With respect, brother,' I say, 'you focus on an irrelevance. How the vision came to me is not the issue. What it portends is vital.'

'What do you think it portends?'

Horror. 'What rage and blood must always mean for the Blood Angels.' I do not need to elaborate. There is a peril ahead aimed at our souls. For that reason, it must be confronted.

'Commander Dante agrees with me that there might be opportunity here too,' says Corbulo. 'A manifestation with such parallels to the Flaw demands our special attention. Your vision makes this doubly true. So how it came to you *is* relevant. Any new symptom is significant. One might be a path to a cure.'

A flash of pity for Corbulo. For the sake of the Chapter, he must hold fast to that hope. He must pursue the quest. I cannot afford that hope. Its loss could doom me utterly. Though I want Corbulo to be correct. He seeks nothing less than the salvation of the Blood Angels.

But salvation is not at hand. Battle is at hand. I pick up my helmet. The void of the skull's eyes gaze back at me. White bones on black. Death and the Rage. I am looking at a mirror. This is my true face. The flesh one is a mask. Its muscles vibrate from strain. To speak is to force my lips back from a snarl. The skin would peel itself away and give the truth free rein.

I don the helmet. I don the skull. But I am not Death. That is the truth of Mephiston. The other holy monster. He is the revenant. I am Rage. I am Doom.

Wearing my identity, I go to find my brothers in madness. Corbulo stays where he is. In this crypt, I am his object of study. Above, a communion awaits that is not for him.

Up a level. A spiral of stone steps. The hollow knell of my boots. I am darkness and crimson. I am rising from the crypt to the asylum.

A long hall before me. Cells on either side. The lighting dim, from torches in sconces before each cell. The flames kept burning by the honour guard that passes once an hour. Flames for the fire of my brothers. For the rage that consumes them, and consumes our enemies. Banners here too, reaching down from the arch keystones. The air just as still as in the crypt, as if the turmoil of sound meant nothing.

The sound means everything. The chorus of wrath. The scream of reason. The unending battle cry of the Death Company. This is the madness of our Chapter. Our tragedy. Our history. We are the Lost, yet we are found in the heart of every Blood Angel. In the grasp of the Black Rage, we do not remember history. We live it. Always. The nightmare of the past, an eternal present. The death of Sanguinius not a scar, but a wound struck again and again, heartbeat by heartbeat.

The betrayal, always. The fall, always. The anguish, always. And the rage, rage, rage for vengeance that can never be enough. The unreachable vengeance sought in every battle. The battles that only I might remember.

I walk down the hall. My tortured brothers hurl themselves against the reinforced doors of their cells. They curse Horus. They will avenge their imprisonment at the hands of Traitors. Their rage is my rage.

The black tendrils creep into my vision. The crimson flickers intensify. My breath becomes ragged.

Blurring.

Such a betrayal. Language dies before it. Rend the Traitors limb from limb. Tear their flesh. There can be no restraint. Feast on their blood.

Is that smoke? Smoke from the walls of the Imperial Palace?

I will–

No.

I am in the hall. I know what is real. But I feel the fury of the past. My soul is on Terra ten thousand years ago. I am one with the heroes of the Death Company. Our rage is our strength. Our strength is our glory, and it is monstrous to behold.

I am a Chaplain. I am the Guardian. I open my mouth and give voice to thunder.

'*Brothers!*'

Silence falls over the Death Company. The Lost attend to me, to madness speaking to madness.

'*We go to war!*'

CHAPTER TWO

Redemption

We go to war in the strike cruiser *Crimson Exhortation*. We go to war in prisons and in chains. As we must.

The other Blood Angels do not fear us, as there is no fear in the hearts of the Adeptus Astartes. They honour us, and our sacrifices. But we are also a source of dread. We are the doom that waits. Any brother who does not fall in battle is fated to join our ranks. We are the end of things. All oaths of moment are steps on the road that leads to the cells. To the howls. To Astorath blade.

We are the force of wrath. We are destruction. We are a terrible weapon, barely contained. The *Crimson Exhortation* travels the immaterium with rage in its hold. When we are unleashed, we will annihilate all in our path.

Corbulo and I are in an interrogation cell. This space is for actual prisoners. Enemies of the Imperium who will be forced to speak the truth. All of it. It is a room devoid of mercy. It is suitable to our needs. To Corbulo's hopes.

There is little light. The ceiling is low. In each of the corners is a sculpture of Sanguinius' face. The gazes intersect at the centre. The Angel's expression is cold. His beauty blank, unforgiving. The object of damnation is a large chair. Its mechanism is capable of perfect justice. We have no need of that today. We do need its restraints. The seat is designed to hold Traitor Marines immobile. It will do the same for me.

I sit down. Corbulo fastens the adamantium shackles to my arms, legs, and forehead. 'Forgive me, Guardian,' he says.

'There is nothing to forgive.' A simple truth. An even simpler one: I am incapable of forgiveness. I know the meaning of the word. I cannot imagine the concept. There is only the Rage. I am only the Rage.

A terrible weapon. Barely contained.

'Then I thank you for your patience,' Corbulo says.

He is wrong about that too. I do what is needed. My duty is my beacon through the darkness of wrath. It keeps me to my path. The Sanguinary High Priest needs my cooperation. So I grant it. The Blood Angels need the hope his work represents. So I will do as I am called upon to nurture that hope.

'We both do what we must,' I say.

'Are you without hope?'

I do not answer. I do not think I can. I would choose to hope, if it were in my power. To escape the Black Rage, to know a singular unity of time and space, that would be a blessing. But only Mephiston has escaped. And what is he that escaped? It was Brother Calistarius who fell. What emerged was something else.

No. I do not hope. To lose hope would hurl me deep into the night of fury.

Corbulo, though, must hope. He must keep searching. If he despairs, the Blood Angels are doomed.

Corbulo moves before me. 'What do you see?' he asks. The signal that the work has begun.

'I see you, Brother Corbulo.'

'Where are we?'

'The lower holds of the *Crimson Exhortation*. Strike cruiser, Fourth Company.'

'Do you understand what we will attempt?'

'Do you?' Impatient. Biting off the words.

'I understand your scepticism, brother.'

Scepticism? Though I am here of my own will, already my limbs are straining against the shackles. My muscles are iron, vibrating with strain. The Black Rage roils at the restraint. I am bound–

Crimson and darkness, writhing.

Bound by treachery.

Destroy the enemy. Spread the wings and strike–

No.

I see Corbulo's face again. He is still speaking. 'We are learning much,' he finishes.

What did he explain? Was there an argument?

Does it matter?

'Proceed,' I say.

He nods. 'We must explore your vision. I will ask you to meditate on it.'

Meditate. There is no better word, perhaps. But it sounds like mockery. Still, I grunt in acknowledgement. I will risk that descent.

'And use my voice as your tether. I am at your side, brother.'

Corbulo believes he has found a key. He must. I doubt. I must, in the impossibility of hope.

'I thank you for your sacrifice,' he says. 'You honour us all.'

I do not answer. I begin the process. The agony. The release of control. Each time, the last moment that I choose to call rational might truly be my last. But my life, my mind and my soul are sworn to the Blood Angels. So I willingly drown.

A wave of exhilarated triumph swamps me. The Black Rage snapping its jaws shut.

Clamour of battle. Laughter of Traitors. The burning Imperium. The Angel falling, falling, falling. The crime calling for revenge, forever.

The fury, forever.

But no, no, no, not this madness.

Flailing. Swimming through blood.

Sinking.

Drowning.

Down.

Down.

Down.

The roar reached Castigon in his quarters. It jolted him from his devotions. The captain of the Knights of Baal rose from his knees. Before him was a small altar, topped with a winged chalice in gold. For a moment, he thought he saw blood pour from its lip. He stood still, listening. He had been deep in prayer, and he wasn't sure if he had really heard the cry. He didn't see how he could have, especially since he knew whose voice it had been.

But there had been something. His spirit was disturbed. He felt as if a war long past echoed just beyond his hearing. The details of his meditation cell were vague. They were insubstantial. Castigon blinked and shook his head. His surroundings settled.

He left his quarters and headed for the lower levels of the *Crimson Exhortation*. He reached the deck where the Death Company was held at the same time as Albinus. The Sanguinary Priest looked as troubled as he felt.

'You heard it too?' Castigon asked.

'Heard...' Albinus hesitated.

'You did, then.'

'I...'

The roar came again. Clearly audible. From the end of the solemn hall before them.

'What is Brother Corbulo doing?'

'It is not my place to question the High Priest,' Albinus said.

No, it wasn't. 'Nor mine,' Castigon admitted. 'But I will.'

I see Horus. The eyes on the black. The Angel at his feet.
  No.
  Horus is not there.
  I see him.
  No. Turn from the ghosts.
  Swim against the current.
  Still drowning.

  Surfacing to a different ghost. A different time. My time. I am the ghost. I am standing. I am addressing my brothers. We are on another ship.

  In orbit around Hadriath XI. We have come to take it back from the orks. I am shouting the words of faith and war. Nobility, pride and inflexibility of purpose: I call on the assembled to embody these precepts. I am in full flight. I am as I once was.

  But I know this moment. The first stumble.

  There is a stir amongst my brothers. Their Chaplain has slipped into High Gothic.

  They see a growing frenzy.

  A double rage takes me. I live the rage I felt then, that initial grip of our bloodline's ghost. The second rage is fresh. Triggered by the knowledge of loss. Remembering what I once was. The anger at the loss of self. The furies feed each other. They compound their damage. Drive me further down.

  Crimson so deep it turns black.

  Echoes of my past. Echoes of the Angel. The cries

of retribution a clamour that fragments all coherent thought.

But I am drowning for a reason.

Fall into the dark, but flail still. Strike at target. Draw blood.

Always more blood. An ocean would not suffice.

An ocean...

Castigon walked towards the interrogation room, Albinus one step behind. On either side, the initiates of the Death Company fought their restraints and threw themselves at the doors of their cells. This was the largest contingent of the Black Rage's victims the *Crimson Exhortation* had transported during Castigon's command of Fourth Company. The scale of the violence that would be unleashed on Phlegethon was immense. Castigon felt a sorrowful awe for his fallen brothers. He knew the pull of the Red Thirst, and the shadow of the Black Rage fell on his soul as it did for all Blood Angels. He practised restraint and prayed for its strength, the better to honour what was most noble in the Chapter's heritage. *We are more than the sum of our curses,* he thought. To fight without restraint, to cut down the enemy with the full force of wrath: there was something there that Castigon almost envied. Almost.

There was nothing to envy in the ravings, though. Nothing to envy in the anguish that shook the stones of the *Exhortation*'s halls. And loudest of all was the booming rasp that came from the interrogation chamber.

But deafening as Lemartes' voice was, how could Castigon have heard it in the upper levels of the superstructure?

He put the question to the side. He knew there would be no satisfactory answers for it. But if he had heard it, and Albinus had, then so had other brothers of the company. Perhaps all had. He could not ignore it.

He reached the door. He looked through its barred aperture. He saw the Sanguinary High Priest engaged in the torture of the Guardian of the Lost.

The ocean in storm. I am there again. The monstrous waves. The sky low, creeping lower. The collision, blood against the solid sky. The figure in the storm. Striding through its works. The bringer of cataclysm.

Essence of rage. Boundless, eternal. The burning blood that will smash the sky.

Something more. Loss?

Loss.

I thrash through my fragments of thought. Desperate to break the ocean's surface, to draw breath, to find reason.

Loss. Whose loss? My loss?

No.

The shadow's loss.

A kernel of knowledge, small but complete. Solid. Absolute. It shines through the rage. I seize it.

Kernel to stone. Stone to anchor. Anchor to real.

Crawling back.

What do I see?

* * *

'I see you, Brother Corbulo.'

Lemartes' voice dropped from a thunder that sought to tear the ship to a whisper as exhausted as it was tense. The change was instantaneous, as if a different being had been teleported into the Chaplain's place. Corbulo straightened and took a step back from where he had been leaning close to Lemartes. He had been calling to the Chaplain for the entirety of the episode. He had been unable to hear his own voice, but Lemartes must have. Something had brought him back, and the fit had been severe.

'I am glad,' Corbulo said. 'You will want...' he began, but stopped himself. He had been going to suggest Lemartes rest. For the Chaplain, the concept had lost all meaning. His jaw was clenched tight. His neck was corded, the tendons iron rods. He had clutched the arms of the chair so hard, his fingers had left indentations. The shackles still held, but if his head had not been restrained as well, if his body had been permitted any leverage at all, Corbulo had no doubt he would have broken free. He would have been loose while in the full grip of delirium.

The question, of course, was whether he was ever free.

Lemartes' gaze locked on him. 'Do you believe I can see you?' Lemartes asked. His eyes were sunken deep into their sockets. They burned with a black flame. His skin was so taut, his face was hardly less of a skull than the death's head that snarled on his helmet.

'Prove to me that you do,' Corbulo said. His demand was not trivial. Lemartes' rationality was not to be taken on trust. If he could speak at all from the other side of the Black Rage, he could be doing so while seeing Corbulo as Horus himself. Lemartes would have to dissemble until he could strike.

Astorath had faith in Lemartes, and that was extraordinary. Corbulo wanted to share that faith. Many in his order had called for the Chaplain's death. Lemartes was an impossibility. The nature of the Flaw meant there could not be a Guardian of the Lost. Only a Redeemer of the Lost. But Astorath disagreed. Astorath stayed his hand. A miracle in itself. There was also the example of Mephiston.

On such beings did the hope of the Chapter lie. And it was his oath to make hope a reality. By any means necessary.

'Proof,' Lemartes said. His breathing was a low, unconscious growl. His eyes shifted to the right of Corbulo's shoulder. 'Castigon is here.'

Corbulo turned around. He saw the captain at the door. He went to open it. Albinus was there as well, his expression carefully neutral. 'You wish to speak to us, brother-captain?' Corbulo asked.

'I have the greatest respect for you and your sacred office,' Castigon said. 'Will you tell me, though, what you are doing to the Chaplain?'

'I believe you are questioning me.'

'I am asking a question. No more than that.'

Castigon, the Lord Adjudicator. Castigon the

politician, Mephiston had called him. Corbulo could see why. At least the captain committed himself to battle with a directness he often avoided in his speech.

Lemartes said, 'He is doing what is necessary.'

'The question is a fair one,' Corbulo said. 'I seek to understand the nature of Chaplain Lemartes' condition. It may hold the key to our Chapter's salvation.'

'Any chance must be taken,' said Lemartes. Iron-clad determination in his voice. 'No matter how remote.' Fatalism just as absolute.

Corbulo was troubled. He had hoped Lemartes would find some reason to have faith in their attempts. They *were* making progress. He had to believe this. There were too many dark alternatives pressing in on the Chapter. If he was wrong about his work with Lemartes, there were other findings that might then be correct, findings he prayed with all the fervour of his soul to be wrong. He held on to what he had gleaned in this session. Hope was hard to come by. Every fragment shone brighter than gold. 'We have a further task,' he said. 'One of immediate import. Chaplain Lemartes has had a vision of the coming mission.'

'That bodes ill,' Castigon said.

That was true. 'Indeed. And so the more we know, the better we can prepare for what awaits us.'

'And what is coming?'

'A powerful force is behind the events on Phlegethon. Commensurate with the scale of the plague.'

'Something more,' said Lemartes. 'There is loss in this rage.'

'As in ours,' Albinus said quietly.

'Yes,' said Corbulo. 'We must be wary of the possible consequences of that similarity.'

Lemartes strained against the shackles. His face contorted. He was briefly a thing of rage and nothing more. Then the spell passed, and his taut rationality returned. 'Different, too. The anger on Phlegethon. It is mindless.'

Castigon nodded. 'I see. This is suggestive, yet I am not sure how to modify tactical decisions in the light of what you have told me.'

'Very true,' Corbulo said. 'We need to know more.'

Castigon winced.

Do you think I take pleasure in this? Corbulo wanted to ask him. *Do you think I delight in my brother's agony?* He said nothing. He could not be seen to hesitate or have doubts.

'Continue,' said Lemartes. His terrible voice of snarl and command filled the chamber. 'Continue,' he said again.

'You have the gratitude of the Knights of Baal,' Castigon said after a moment. He seemed disgusted with his own platitude. But there was nothing else he could say. He turned away and walked off.

Albinus didn't follow right away. To Corbulo he said, 'I wish you strength and wisdom.'

'Thank you, brother.' The other Sanguinary Priest could see the toll that the sessions took on him. The thought that his efforts might be pointless, that he treated Lemartes like a specimen in a laboratorium, was itself a torture.

Corbulo shut the cell door as Albinus followed Castigon. There was no practical reason for closing off the space. There were no secrets here. The door was not locked. And it did nothing to contain the roars of the Chaplain.

Corbulo turned back to his task.

His subject glared back at him. '*Continue.*'

The hiss of rage and sacrifice.

The rage had spread from Hive Profundis to Hive Corymbus. The hundreds of kilometres of plains between the two hives swarmed with millions seeking an enemy for their wrath. They found it in the 237th Siege Regiment of the Mordian Iron Guard, commanded by Colonel Iklaus Reinecker. A phalanx of cold discipline marched in gold-brocaded blue uniforms.

Inside *Guardian of Kulth*, Reinecker's command Chimera, Lieutenant Mannchen said, 'If we weren't here, they might just kill themselves off.'

Reinecker was about to climb through the Chimera's hatch. He rounded on his adjutant. 'So we should abandon our mission? Turn tail from the mobs?'

Mannchen looked as if he wanted to take a step back, but there was nowhere for him to retreat in the cramped confines of the *Guardian*. 'Of course not, colonel.'

'Good. You're lucky Commissar Stromberg didn't hear those words.'

'Forgive me, I–'

'We are here,' Reinecker continued. 'Where we should be. We are here to impose order on this planet, and I will be damned the day I live to see the Emperor's will enforced simply because we stood by and let a population wipe itself out. You would do well to remember that the southern continent is still free of this infection. Or would you have us abandon it to heretical madness?'

'I apologise, colonel,' Mannchen tried again. 'I was speaking out of frustration.'

Reinecker grunted and climbed through the hatch. *Guardian* was in the front ranks of the Mordian advance, with only a wedge of Leman Russ tanks before it. The progress was slow, the armoured vehicles barely moving faster than the infantry. Reinecker snatched up a vox handset. 'All forward tanks,' he transmitted. 'Accelerate. I want to be at the gates of Profundis by nightfall.'

The hive's bulk dominated the horizon, its details blurred with distance. It was still fifty kilometres away.

The initial landings had gone well. Orbital bombardments had cleared the target area of the enemy. Reinecker had picked a low plateau, broad enough to deploy the company while providing high ground for the start of the campaign. It was also within striking distance of Profundis, which was the epicentre of the plague. Picts captured by reconnaissance flights beneath the cloud cover showed crowd movements like the spiral of a great storm, with the hive as the eye. The mob from Corymbus flowed straight into the vortex of Profundis, as if caught by the greater gravitational force. As the reports had continued to come in during the landings, Reinecker noticed an odd ebb and flow to the mob. It seemed to contract, the people drawn back to the hive for reasons unknown, before expanding outwards with renewed violence, swallowing up the farms and smaller cities.

Profundis, then, was the key. There was not a question of a simple disease of the mind, an infection that was spreading along random vectors. There was an impetus behind the rage, an ongoing one, and it kept renewing the strength of the mob. If the Mordians took the city, they would stab the uprising in the heart.

The 237th rolled down from the plateau, driving a wide swath through the enemy. Heavy armour in the lead, a huge, mechanised scythe. The infantry followed in its wake. The foot soldiers would kill many more of the enemy, but against millions on open terrain, their effectiveness was limited. Reinecker planned to use their strength at Profundis itself, when there would be a focus for the assault.

The first hour of the advance went as he planned. The company ate up the kilometres. The Mordians flattened the enemy. But then the mob converged with ever greater numbers. And it fought harder than

Reinecker had expected. He knew these people were mad. And still they surprised him. Unarmed civilians ran straight at Leman Russ tanks. They never retreated. Not even orks showed such a complete absence of the instinct for self-preservation.

The company's speed dropped.

Most of the mob was unarmed, except with makeshift melee weapons: blades and tools and clubs made from bits of wreckage. They could do nothing to the Mordians except crowd in to die. But the Phlegethon Nightwatch militia was in the fight too. And as the company drew the wrath to itself, the Nightwatch killed their way through the civilians to make their assault on the invaders. Their arsenal was inferior to the Mordians', but they could not be ignored.

Slower still.

And so Reinecker was at the hatch, to see the battle for himself, and to urge the tanks forward.

The people of Phlegethon pressed in on the company's formation from all sides. They were a wave, a wall, a fevered boil of maggots. Reinecker wasn't sure whether to regard them as heretics or lunatics, or something else again. They fought as if diseased, and yet for all its mindlessness, the rage was a passion. The berserk were bloodied, their flesh and clothing torn. They foamed at the mouth, and their anger was so extreme that it robbed them of language. But they were still recognisably human. They had not undergone the rotting transformation that afflicted the victims of the Plague of Unbelief. Though their frenzy seemed as if it would tear their bodies apart from within, they knew how to use weapons. The militia even used formations.

He knew his order to the heavy armour was a risk. It would outdistance the infantry. But he was sure the discipline and the firepower of his soldiers was more than enough to beat back the mob. A gradual advance would only give time for more and more millions to close in.

Ahead, in answer to his command, the engines roared. Heavy bolter turrets fired continuously. But the tanks did not accelerate. And the cannons were silent.

'Front ranks,' Reinecker voxed, 'I told you to accelerate.'

'We are, colonel,' Sergeant Penkert replied. 'The enemy is stopping us.'

'How?' There were no enemy vehicles.

'Numbers.' Penkert sounded nonplussed.

Reinecker cursed. 'Make a hole,' he ordered. Then he spoke to Katscher, who was steering *Guardian*. 'Take us forward.'

The tanks ahead shifted to the left and right, and Katscher drove the Chimera up the gap, advancing the last hundred metres to the front. Reinecker's jaw dropped. Penkert was right – numbers alone were blocking the advance. The wave of raging humanity was breaking against the tanks, and it kept coming. The vehicles were trying to push against a solid wall of flesh that extended, from what Reinecker could see, all the way to the gates of Hive Profundis. The people clawed and trampled each other in their compulsion to kill the Mordians. The frenzy on the flanks of the company's formation was paltry by comparison.

For the moment.

Reinecker re-evaluated his strategy. If the crowd built up to this point on all sides, it would be enough to crush the Iron Guard.

The first line of tanks had formed their own wall. There was no space between them. Bolter turrets shredded the crowd, but individuals squeezed through, water through a cracking dyke. The big guns were unusable. They were buried in the wave. Point-blank shots into that mass would be disastrous.

'Full stop,' Reinecker ordered. 'Wyverns, I want a walking barrage, beginning one hundred metres forward of our front lines. Fire until further order. Hellhounds, move to second rank and stand by to take first.'

A few moments passed. Over the howling wind-roar of the mob's anger, the sounds of the battle were the shriek of las-fire exchanged between the Iron Guard and the Nightwatch, the staccato barks of bolters, and the growl of engines as the tanks jockeyed for positions. There was little room to do so and preserve the integrity of the column, but Reinecker's drivers had performed finer manoeuvres in the more confined spaces of urban battles. The Leman Russ variants pulled back as the Hellhounds moved forward.

Then came the greater wind. It was the steel exhalation of the Wyverns firing their twin-linked stormshard mortars, a *hoom hoom hoom hoom* heralding the death to come. There were multiple launches, so close together they could have been a single one. The shells arced over the column. They rose skyward, and when they dropped, they raced to the ground with hungry shrieks, their pitch so sharp it cut though the crowd's rage with a blade. Reinecker counted the seconds from launch. 'Now,' he said, at the precise moment of the airburst.

A storm of shrapnel hundreds of metres wide tore into the crowd. It turned the terrain before the company into an abattoir. For several seconds, there was no air. There was only the flight of razored metal, so dense and all-consuming it was indistinguishable from the smoke of the explosions. Reinecker heard screams, human ones. They were brief. But they were the mark of a force more powerful than rage.

And the force kept coming. The *hoom hoom hoom hoom* of the launches continued, and then the steel whistle of the dropping shells. Then explosions further ahead, flashes in the murk, and the screams of shrapnel and flesh. More smoke, spreading over the battlefield, smothering with the stench of fyceline.

Reinecker smiled. He breathed the acrid smoke, savouring it. 'Hellhounds,' he voxed, 'lead us forward. Scorch the earth.'

The Hellhounds moved, and *Guardian* went with them, one rank back. The column entered the hell of its own creation. Profundis disappeared behind the pall. The day turned into roiling, shifting twilight. The terrain was a shadowy unevenness of chewed-up ground and a mire of blood and body pieces. The Hellhounds sent a stream of fire forward, baking the ground, turning corpses into ash, incinerating the enemy who rushed into the gap.

The Wyverns kept launching. The barrage marched ahead, leaving footprints of slaughter. Reinecker waited until he judged a full kilometre had been scoured of life. Even the pressure on the flanks had eased as the smoke and wounds ate into the mob's physical ability to fight.

'Good work, Wyverns,' Reinecker said. 'Sporadic fire for now. We'll see what we can do with the momentum you've bought us. Infantry, forced march. I want those gates to fall by dawn.'

He felt a breeze against his face as the vehicles picked up speed. He was not a man given to smiling, but he did now. Then his vox-operator was calling for his attention, and he ducked back down the hatch, closing it behind him.

'What is it, Adra?'

'Communication from the *Vanandra*, colonel. A vessel has transitioned into the system.'

'Get me Admiral Kupfer.'

Adra nodded and sat back down at the vox.

The Blood Angels had arrived, Reinecker guessed. Sooner than he had expected. He would have wished to be closer to his goal before now. He knew the

Chapter had been alerted, and the scale of the crisis warranted their presence. But once they were here, the glory of victory would go to them. The role of the Mordian Iron Guard would become a footnote in the histories of the war, if it were mentioned at all. Reinecker did not believe he was reckless in the quest for glory. But he saw no reason to turn from the opportunity for the laurel wreath. He pressed his lips together. The war could not be won before the Blood Angels made planetfall. But he would break through into Profundis. He could promise himself that much.

He squeezed into his seat before the tacticarium table while he waited for Adra to establish communication with the commander of the Dictator-class cruiser. He felt the Chimera jounce over the rough terrain. Some of those bumps, it pleased him to think, were mounds of the shredded, incinerated enemies of the Imperium, now ground flat by *Guardian of Kulth*'s treads. 'Katscher,' he called to the driver, 'are you taking us over or through our good work?'

'Both, colonel,' she answered from her cramped compartment. 'Over their mud and through their ash.'

The speed felt good. There would be heavy fighting ahead, but he felt he had the measure of the foe. The 237th would prosecute its war with precision. He would show the Adeptus Astartes what the unenhanced human could do. Not the common human, though. No such thing had ever been born on Mordian.

Reinecker frowned at the vox-operator. 'What's taking so long, trooper?' he asked.

'I don't know, sir,' Adra said, puzzled.

'Atmospheric interference?' He thought about the smoke and the thickening smog cover as they approached the hive.

Adra shook his head. 'I had them, and then I didn't. There was no fading of the transmission.'

'Let me hear over the 'caster.'

Adra toggled a switch. There was an electrical crackle from the vox-caster. Adra hailed the *Vanandra* several times. Nothing came back. Even in the rattling din of the *Guardian*'s interior, the silence from the cruiser was large, clean. Reinecker grew uneasy.

'Keep trying,' he said.

He went back up the hatch. He wanted to experience the sight and sound of the war going well.

Smoke and thunder surrounded him. The air was sharp with spent fyceline and burning promethium. Before him, the flames of the Hellhounds lit the gloom with violent glows. The Wyverns were still launching, but more sparingly, with long beats between the arcing death. The Leman Russ battle tanks now had the space to use their guns. Some fired to the front, their shells' blasts almost invisible in the distance, though Reinecker knew they were hitting their targets. Unless the mob had suddenly changed tactic, there was no possible way to miss.

On the flanks, the armour was hitting the enemy

hard as well. The Exterminator variants pounded the tide of anger with their autocannons. The mob still pressed forward, and the Nightwatch still returned fire, but they were making no progress. Reinecker used the company vox to check with officers down the length of the column. Casualties were light.

You do not lay siege to us, Reinecker thought. *Not to the 237th. That is our privilege.*

He would demonstrate that truth to the enemy even more forcefully soon. Hive Profundis was drawing closer. He could see the bulk of its shadow through the smoke now.

An hour passed. Reinecker stayed in his position. He watched the shape of the hive gather definition. The column's progress was steady, unwavering. The Iron Guard had become a juggernaut. The rage of millions was pitiful before its might.

But there was still no word from the *Vanandra.* Nor from the other ship. The sight of war perfectly waged wasn't enough to quell Reinecker's growing unease. He resisted the impulse to ask Adra for non-existent information. Instead, he trained the heavy bolter, firing into the gaps between tanks on the left flank, biting into the infinite sea of frenzied humanity.

Night was falling. And then it wasn't. The sky glared white. Reinecker winced. He looked up through the smoke. The cloud cover pulsed with light from explosions. Lightning without thunder. Reinecker stared. Denial rose from his chest, but his throat was suddenly dry, and he couldn't even form the word *no.*

The light faded. Night returned, but only briefly. Then day fell. Day came down in great fragments, a rain of comets trailing parallel tails of fire. Day was shattered, yet still massive. Some of the pieces of day came down mere kilometres from the column, and now there was thunder, and a great shaking of the earth.

And more light. The last of it. Expanding fireballs from the hundred deaths of the *Vanandra*.

Reinecker released the bolter. He fumbled with the vox handset. He swallowed three times before he could speak. 'Continue the advance,' he ordered. 'Be ready for a new enemy.' There was nothing else to say. The company's commissars would take care of morale. They would be shouting, no doubt, that what they had seen changed nothing. That they were warriors of the Iron Guard, and they would repay in full the insult they had just suffered.

An insult. He almost laughed at the thought. The destruction of a cruiser was certainly an insult. It was also, he knew, a death sentence. There would be no glory for him and the 237th today. There would be annihilation.

Reinecker faced forward, wanting to see the worst when it arrived. *Continue the advance,* he thought. There was nothing else to do. And if glory was impossible on this day, at least there would be honour.

The column rolled on for another hour. The light of the *Vanandra*'s death faded to a dirty glow where brush fires had caught. The mortar shells kept falling, the jets of flaming promethium held the way clear, and the beat of the cannons continued. For that hour, the Mordian Iron Guard marched on as if to victory. Nothing could stop the company's advance. The fall of the ship was a bad dream.

Annihilation came as the leading vehicles of the column approached the mud plain surrounding Hive Profundis. *Guardian of Kulth* was passing between the ruins of farm buildings when Reinecker saw large, blunt-nosed shapes descend from the clouds. 'Thunderhawks,' he warned. He had a moment of desperate, irrational hope. He stared at the gunships, as if they might miraculously reveal the colours of the Blood Angels.

They did not. No crimson, only black and brass. And then more streaks broke away from the Thunderhawks – Assault Space Marines with jump packs.

'Fire on the ships!' Reinecker shouted, and the cannons were already changing their orientation.

No glory, but honour: a Leman Russ of the Mordian Iron Guard got a shot off before the Thunderhawks unleashed their rockets.

CHAPTER THREE

Bringer of Miracles

The void over Phlegethon crackles with aftermath. We have missed an engagement by very little. The auspex array of the *Crimson Exhortation* picks up residual radiation, the signatures of dissipating plasma. The oculus shows the tumble of debris, both rocky and metallic. Not the flotsam of Phlegethon's cloud of moonlets. The trace of a great death.

I stand in the bridge's strategium with Corbulo and Castigon. The tacticarium screens are being updated by new picts as we collect data on the war unfolding below. Heat blooms detectable through the cloud atmosphere hint at the deployment of forces on the surface. We have established vox-contact with Colonel Reinecker. We have a picture of a siege gone wrong. We have a picture of our true enemy.

The Blood Disciples. We know little about them, but

we do know what they were. They were the Eighth Company of the Emperor's Wolves, led by Captain Khevrak. They were loyal to the Emperor, and then they fell to rage. There are lessons and parallels here. I should seek to understand them. Once I might have. But there are Traitors below–

Below, on Terra. The Palace under siege. The Traitor Legions wait for justice. Spread the wings of war. Bring fire and blood to Horus.

No.

Not Terra. Phlegethon. But yes, there are Traitors.

I can think only of their bloody end. Every moment I am not killing them is a torture.

My hands are fists forever. The tendons in my arms have turned to iron from the effort to remain conscious of the present.

The hololith on the table before us adjusts to take in the most recent information. Castigon points to the area before the western gates of Hive Profundis. 'The Blood Disciples have established a strongpoint there. Two thousand metres separates them from the current position of the Iron Guard.' He indicates ground further to the west, slightly higher than the flatness before the hive. 'It seems that the entire population of Profundis is lost to the blood frenzy.'

'We should not expect to free them of its grip,' Corbulo says.

'Agreed. Extermination will be a mercy. That will fall to the 237th, once they are free to act again.'

'The situation is a stalemate?' I ask.

'Attrition,' says Castigon. 'It is fortunate that this is a siege company. The Mordians' heavy armour has been enough to keep them in the fight this long.'

Even so. 'They are fighting well,' I say. They are against a force millions strong and a warband of Traitor Space Marines. To have survived at all is an achievement.

'There is also this,' says Castigon. He magnifies the image on one of the pict screens. The Traitor ship. It is also a strike cruiser. And its name is disturbing: *Ira Sanguinem*. Mirrors and echoes. Madness reflected.

We will be tested down below.

'The enemy vessel is embedded deep within the moon cluster,' Castigon explains. 'Manoeuvring to that position would have been very risky. But its defensive position is now excellent.'

It is surrounded by rocky shields. I turn my attention away from the screen. I will not be boarding that vessel. I will not be killing Traitors there. I will be at war below. I hold myself in check. I am not at war yet. I am not in battle yet.

'Defence is an odd tactical choice for this warband,' Corbulo says.

'They are all below.' I am sure of this truth. Their vessel has seen its use here. Their full attention is planetside. Something calls to them. I think it might call to us.

The test has already begun. My impatience grows. Castigon nods. He looks thoughtful.

Enough! To arms! My rage scraping to the surface. My

brothers in the strategium are moving as if underwater. Decisions being made at leisure. Movements slow, pensive.

Enough! There are Traitors!

I turn to look at the oculus. Phlegethon turns below. My vision doubles. I see Terra too. A ghost over a corpse.

I know the difference. I do. But war comes. War calls. Vengeance calls.

The difference blurs.

Castigon chose the southern region of the mud flat as the staging area. The terrain was wide open and level. It was also covered by a solid mass of the wrathful.

The Blood Angels exterminated them.

The drop pods came down first. The decelerating blast of the retro-rockets scorched the mortals below. Then came the impact, killing dozens more. The enemy was already reeling before the pods opened, lethal blossoms, and unleashed their cargos of battle-brothers. The Blood Angels took to the field. The initial squads arrived with a heavy complement of flamers. They sent out sheets of cleansing fire. Before the landers arrived with the first of the heavy vehicles, mere minutes after the drop pods hit, the enemy casualties were in the thousands. The landing zone was still far from clear. That was expected. The landers came down, adding their engines and mass to the massacre.

Corbulo was in the first of the drop pods. He wanted

to see the frenzy up close. The patterns that were developing in this war disturbed him. He had to discern their meaning before they became traps. If it wasn't already too late. There was much more that he should be seeing here. His perception felt blunted, as if the pattern was too large to be grasped. But he would look, and he would learn, and so he confronted the mortals' rage directly. He did not use a flamer. He left his bolt pistol maglocked to his belt. But he did carry Heaven's Teeth high, the holy chainsword growling its hatred for the wretches that charged at him.

There was nothing they could do against the power that descended upon them. Their numbers here were dropping quickly. The Blood Angels were killing them faster than their comrades in madness could arrive. But still they attacked, more single-minded and unheeding than any beast.

Corbulo grabbed the first that closed with him by the tunic. He lifted the man to eye level, ignoring the other attacks. His prisoner scrabbled at him, spitting, gagging on his own fury. Corbulo looked into the mortal's eyes. Was there anything familiar in this madness? Because he hoped, to the core of his soul, that there was not, he forced himself to look hard. There was nothing left of the individual. The thing he held was a flesh automaton. The body was a vehicle for wrath, and that was all. Corbulo hadn't expected to see any echo of the Black Rage. Perhaps there were some similarities with the Red Thirst. They were surface ones, though.

'We have nothing to learn from you,' Corbulo said to the wretch, and prayed that he spoke the truth. He hurled the man to the ground. He acknowledged the others now, mobbing him, trying to kill him with their numbers and their hate. He brought Heaven's Teeth down and swept the chainsword in an arc. Heads flew, their faces frozen in their final snarls.

He cut through the wrathful with every step. He continued his examination. He kept looking for meaning. He saw none, unless that absence was itself meaningful. He didn't stop until the tanks were ready.

Corbulo approached the lead vehicle. It was a Baal Predator, and its name stopped him cold. It was the *Phlegethon*. It had last seen action on Pallevon. It was named for this world, where the Blood Angels had fought once before, so many thousands of years ago. They had brought Phlegethon into compliance.

More of the pattern. More omens.

Something was approaching, but he could not see it.

He boarded the tank.

As dawn broke, smudged brown light replacing the darkness, the column moved out. It moved fast. And as it neared the Mordians' position, the air attack began.

Two formations. On the ground the tanks and our brothers on foot make for the besieged Iron Guard. From above we take the war to the enemy strongpoint. The Stormravens *Bloodthorn*, *Cruentus* and

Grail of War carry the Death Company. We are thirty. In my squad is Quirinus, the latest of the fallen. The great Reclusiarch, his horror of Mephiston such that he embraced the Black Rage when it fell on him. Corbulo sees hope in his fall. He sees the hint of choice. I do not. Quirinus was weak. And he was doomed.

As are we all, our crimson armour now black as our fate. We are the doomed, and we bring doom. The side doors of the *Bloodthorn* are open. Wind tears through the interior of the gunship. It carries smoke, blood, the call of war. At a moment's notice, we will attack. On the right flank of our squadron are three Thunderhawks. Castigon is aboard the *Primarch's Wings*.

The squadrons come in low, through dense smoke. The hive is burning. Before its gates are the Traitors. They do not have many tanks. Two Predators face west, supported by two Rhinos. Blood Disciples form a line behind them. They guard a mound of wreckage. Atop it, a human gesticulates. His movements seize my attention. The black web at the edge of my vision convulses. The field swims red. Rage speaks to rage. The man is still a distant insect, but his gestures resonate as if made by a Titan. Each one is a jab and a goad.

flicker strobe blur
He is a preacher...
black red black red black red
No...
burning ramparts of Terra, falling Angel, the cries of absolute loss

He is a prophet.

Around me, the brothers of the Death Company shout. They are unshackled and armed. They could tear the *Bloodthorn* apart in an instant. But they follow me, their Chaplain. Their guardian. Their comrade in the hell of blood memory. They listen because we share a reality. As battle nears, this remembered war becomes insistent for me. It begins to displace the one perceived by the other Blood Angels, the ones who still walk in the light of hope.

But this man. He has been in my sight for seconds. I can feel his power. So does the mob. The currents below us are in response to his gestures. The effects are more pronounced closest to him, where he can be seen and heard. He pulls his arms in, and the people rush forward. He thrusts outward, and the flock storms to the west. They are his puppets. My brothers and I feel the yank of the strings too.

Yet his movements are angular, jagged. He too is pulled. He is slave to another's will.

'Brother-captain,' I vox. Speaking to this reality is difficult. 'The preaching mortal. He is the primary threat. Target him.'

No response.

The *Bloodthorn* dips. The loss of altitude is sudden. Our flight weaves for no reason. Except in answer to the gestures of the preacher. 'Brother Orias?' I vox to the pilot. Silence. I shout his name again.

'Yes, Chaplain,' Orias answers. There is a rasp in his breath. The *Bloodthorn* stabilises.

That mortal affects us all. The possibility that he might plunge the entirety of the Fourth into the illusion of the Death Company occurs to me. The thought fills me with horror.

I vox to the whole squadron. I repeat the names of pilots and of Castigon. I am calling them to the real. The irony is dark, and we are seconds from disaster. The other gunships are flying erratically. The *Cruentus* veers towards us. Orias pulls us up. We can avoid collision, but the *Cruentus* is angling towards the ground. It will hit at full speed.

The Blood Disciples fire on us. The cannons of the Predators flash. Rockets streak our way. A squadron of three enemy Thunderhawks rises from behind the gates of Profundis.

'*Hear me!*' I command, rage countering rage.

I am heard. Reality falls over the squadron again. Gunships evade and return fire. The *Cruentus* is not fast enough. A rocket strikes its starboard wing. The ship veers. Its engines scream. Trailing smoke, it drops lower, but straightens.

Our rockets and autocannon shells strike the enemy positions. Our accuracy has been compromised while we struggle to free ourselves of the net cast by the preacher's mesmerising incantation. Scores of humans die in the blasts. A Rhino erupts in flame, but the Traitor at its turret keeps firing.

The mortal on his throne of wreckage exults. He gestures. He commands the flight of the Traitor gunships. They ignore us, and fly west, towards the Iron Guard.

Through the breaking *black red black red black red* storm in my vision and my mind, a thought clamours for attention: *what mortal is this who commands Space Marines?*

Castigon speaks. Strain in his voice, but clear. 'Chaplain Lemartes, intercept those gunships.'

Our squadrons split up. The Thunderhawks curve around for a second attack run. The Stormravens roar towards the enemy.

The shouting of my brothers is deafening. They know battle is here. They cry for vengeance and honour. They will save Terra. They will avenge the Angel. Each is lost in his own nightmare of the past. I am with them all. And we are together. And we know whom to strike. We are the Blood Angels who have lost everything. We are a horror of war.

Our flight angles away from the Blood Disciples' base. The prophet recedes from view. His grip weakens. Orias is on the vox with the other pilots. The *Bloodthorn*'s course is strong and true.

The Stormravens are faster than the Thunderhawks. We converge with the enemy squadron at a point midway across the plain. The insects struggle below us. They reach up in frustrated anger. They would pull us from the sky.

Now.

'*For Sanguinius!*' I shout. My brothers roar back.

I haul back and lean out the side door. Wind and smoke storm through the compartment. The gunships have set the sky aflame. They streak through the filthy atmosphere for each other. My ears fill with the chorus of roars: engines, guns, explosions and the rush of air.

Orias opens up against the lead Thunderhawk with the *Bloodthorn*'s assault cannons.

Jump packs ignite as we leap.

From all three Stormravens, furies clad in night streak from the side doors. The enemy Thunderhawks cannot outrun and cannot evade. They return fire, maintain their course towards the Iron Guard, and unleash their own assault troops.

We clash in the air.

Red fills my vision.

The wars of the present and past become one.

On the ground, the Blood Angels rolled over and through the wrathful. The Baal Predators were at the head of the column. Their flamestorm cannons turned the mob into a sea of fire. The siege shields scraped the dead, the burning and the struggling from the ground. Soon they were pushing forward mounds of smouldering corpses. Corbulo rode in the open hatch of the *Phlegethon*. He watched the tank turn the people of the world in whose name it had been baptised into ash and dust. He didn't see war. He saw a needed extinction. There was no salvation for the infected. If the southern continent of Phlegethon were not still communicating, and if the Iron Guard weren't bogged down, he would have argued in favour of Exterminatus.

As the *Phlegethon* approached the 237th Regiment, Corbulo heard the exchange of fire. The Mordians were besieged. The mob surrounded them on all sides. Many of the wrathful here wore the uniform of the defence militia, and rained las-fire on the Guard. To the east, at the furthest point that the regiment had advanced, squads of the Blood Disciples were grinding their way through the Mordians.

The Iron Guard had been hit hard by the Traitors. If the Blood Disciples had not divided their force, more intent on holding on to their position at the gates, Corbulo thought the regiment might already be lost. Much of the heavy armour had been destroyed. Caught in the open, the Mordians had reacted well. They had turned their wounds into a stronghold. Burned and smashed vehicles formed a wall around their position. The barrier was a tangle of agonised metal. The tanks that were still intact pushed between the gaps and blasted the enemy. If they were destroyed, they would still serve in death. The wall was an act of battlefield improvisation that impressed Corbulo. Its creation would have required a miraculous combination of a commander's inspiration and the crew's skill to manoeuvre into the needed positions even as the worst was happening.

The Blood Angels came in at the south-eastern point of the wall. The Blood Disciples did not turn from their attack until the last moment. They were all assault troops. Their jump packs took them over the wall and into the midst of the Iron Guard, and then out again. Hit and run, again and again. Corbulo counted twenty Traitors. Twenty against thousands. They would have been enough.

But not now.

'Warriors of Mordian!' Sergeant Gamigin vox-cast from inside the *Phlegethon*. 'You have fought well. You have held the enemy. Now we bring the reckoning!'

There was no cheer from the Mordians. Such an expression was not in their nature. Instead, there was a surge of fire directed at the Blood Disciples. Pressed to the limit, the Iron Guard rallied, and showed their gratitude by fighting still harder.

Assault cannons and storm bolter turrets on the Predators and Land Raiders reached out for the Blood Disciples. The vehicles slowed, letting the tactical squads move forward and add their bolters to the barrage. The tank gunners held back from using the lascannons, which would have destroyed the Iron Guard defences. The Blood Disciples were fast, changing the arc of their assaults to close with the column. The hail of shells hit them. Two vanished, struck full by salvoes of assault cannon shells, their jump packs detonating. Others were wounded, landing awkwardly a short distance from the column. The rest, their own bolters spitting shells, came down behind the lead tanks.

One landed on the rear of the *Phlegethon*. Corbulo leapt out of the hatch as bolter shells stitched their way up the centre of the tank. He fired back with his bolt pistol. He hit the Traitor in the chest plate. Armour smoking, the Disciple staggered back a step, then charged forward, firing again. Corbulo crouched low. Shells whistled over his head. He lunged with Heaven's Teeth. The blade plunged into the Disciple's damaged armour. The sword growled, teeth cutting through ceramite to punish the flesh. The Traitor tried to pull free. The chainblade had him. Corbulo pushed harder, ground through carapace and bone. The Disciple fired his bolter, tried to bring it around to Corbulo's face. The Sanguinary Priest smashed his arm away and drove the sword home to the Disciple's hearts.

Gunfire in the midst of the column. The Blood Disciples engaged long enough to change the focus of the battle, then jumped out again. They lost three more.

Corbulo heard the roar of gunships. *They distracted us,* he thought. *They held us still.*

Thunderhawks closed in over the mud plain. But Blood Angels Stormravens were on an intercept course. Jump-packed warriors shot out of both squadrons of gunships.

The cannons of the battle tanks swivelled. Turrets were already firing.

A perfect convergence of foes.

But then, on the other side of the plain, another event. Massive. Terrible.

It seized Corbulo's gaze. It filled him with horror.

Khevrak stood with his brothers at the foot of the hill of wreckage. Above him, the Prophet of Blood raged with truth. The sounds coming from his throat were not words. They were an invocation, and they were much more than that. They were the will of the Blood God speaking directly to the souls of the faithful, and they were the worship of his fury given a form more true than any hymn. They were wrath carved out of air. There was no meaning, no inadequacy of language to betray the force and the purity. Even as his blood boiled with the intensity of sublime rage, and his mind turned molten with the anticipation of perfect violence, Khevrak also mourned. This was what he and his brothers had lost centuries ago when the Emperor's Wolves Eighth Company had completed their final task for the false god. This was what they could have had. Their journey to transcendence had been delayed by their great error.

But they had paid their penance. Their redemption was at hand. The Prophet was weaving a great work. The madness of hundreds of millions was its material. The Prophet's cries built and built, his throat surpassing the human. He never drew breath now. No howls ever stopped. Layers upon layers of new ones were added. The exponential shriek would soon be greater than the sum of its millions of stolen parts.

Even then, would that be enough? Khevrak had faith it would be. But didn't he hear his loss echoed in the cry too? The cry was without meaning, yet it was laden with enough to shatter worlds. Was it the regret of his brothers woven into the work? He did not think so. It was a greater loss yet.

He would know soon. Revelation was coming. All that was required was that the Prophet complete his work.

So he kept the bulk of his force in reserve. For the first time in the history of the warband, the Blood Disciples fought to protect. This weak vessel must not be harmed. The crime of their birth must not be repeated. He sent enough of his strength to stop the Mordians. Now the Blood Angels, deniers of the gift of wrath, were here. They would experience revelation too. Perhaps the Blood God would redeem them as well. If not, then they would die.

The Thunderhawks flew off, drawing the focus of the battle away from the Prophet.

Soon, very soon.

'Do you feel it, captain?' Dhassaran asked, his voice a hiss of ecstatic fury.

'I do, Apostle. I do.' A barrier was about to be breached. A culmination was upon them. The mass of rage from the population of the hive, from the deaths in the conflagrations in the hive itself, and from the waging of the war, reached critical mass.

Above, Blood Angels Thunderhawks were closing in. Their first run had done little. Khevrak had seen their flight disrupted by the will of the Prophet. The second was coming in hard and fast. 'Take them down!' he ordered.

And then he felt it. The breach.

'No need!' Dhassaran said, and the power of the moment tore a sound from the Dark Apostle that was a bellow of laughter and a howl of fulfilled rage.

Khevrak joined him. So did all his Disciples. They had moved beyond redemption.

This was rapture.

A short distance beyond their defensive perimeter, the land answered the Prophet's sermon. It shook. It cracked. It tore itself open. And the miracle of the Blood Disciples' birth returned.

CHAPTER FOUR

The Pillar

'Rockets to that mound of rubble,' Castigon ordered as the squadron wheeled around to begin the attack. 'Do not look at that mortal. Acknowledge.'

The pilots of the other Thunderhawks confirmed. Good. Lemartes was right. That small figure was the greatest threat. In the cockpit beside Agares, Castigon averted his gaze from the man's unholy dance. It took a great effort. The pull of those gestures was massive. Castigon was fighting the gravitational tug of a spiritual black hole.

'Fly true, brother,' he said to Agares.

'I will, captain.' Agares spoke with the same strain Castigon felt in his own voice.

Is this, he wondered, *what every second of consciousness is like for Lemartes?*

'Anger wants to take us,' he said over the company

vox, speaking to all and to himself. 'Do not let it. Remember that we are more than our rage.'

The squadron's flight was true.

Reality stumbled. The ground between the gunships and the target split. People fell into the widening crevasse. The densely packed mob around it began to swirl. The movement became a vortex. Within seconds, there was a spin of thousands, moving at whirlwind speeds. The vortex contracted even as it captured more and more and more bodies. They flew. They formed a tornado of flesh. It shot up from the ground, ten metres high, twenty, fifty. Agares banked the Thunderhawk hard. The gunship shook. It resisted his commands and vectored back towards the funnel.

A hundred metres high now, and still contracting.

'Shoot it,' Castigon ordered.

Agares fired. All the gunships did. Thunderhawk cannons, hellstrike missiles, lascannons and heavy bolters poured their fury into the monstrous wonder. Perhaps they completed the horror. Perhaps the crushing density of the contraction was enough. No matter the reason, the flesh vanished. The bodies burst. Blood exploded from the core of the twister. It raced to the base and to its full height.

Twisting, roaring, a pillar of blood reached for the sky. The movements of its length were sinuous. It bent and straightened. It was the dance of the prophet enacted at the highest level. It was eruption and storm and call.

It spun out spiral arms of blood. They fell on the mob. They lashed against the squadron.

Crimson slammed into the *Primarch's Wings'* canopy. The armourglass shattered. The blood fell on Castigon and Agares.

The gunship fell, spinning.

Castigon didn't notice. For him, there was only the Thirst.

I am a spear. I am justice. I am these things because I am rage. My flight is a meteor streak from the *Bloodthorn*. My focus on the target is unwavering. The Blood Disciples Thunderhawk is the centre of my sight and my reality. Around it, the worlds interleave. I am on Phlegethon, and on Terra. I am in the shadow of Hive Profundis, and of the Imperial Palace. Time flickers back and forth over ten thousand years. I am in one era, then the other, both, neither.

The jagged black, the pulsing crimson.

Reality is broken. It is lies. All that matters is my target. What must die is clear. My enemy is the enemy of the Emperor, the betrayer of the Angel and his promise. The red and the black obscure all that is not my prey. All that will not fall to my rage.

The *Bloodthorn* is higher than the nearest Thunderhawk when I leap. As I descend, a Blood Disciple rises to confront me. I fly with bolt pistol in my right hand. My left holds the Blood Crozius. In the uncertain wavering of time, the relic is my great anchor. It is solid. It existed ten thousand years ago as truly as it does now. It glowed scarlet when it was wielded by the first High Chaplain of the Blood Angels. It glows for me now. It killed then. It kills now.

The Traitor thinks to stop me. I do not alter my flight. I swing the Blood Crozius as we collide. The winged head of the Crozius has a blunt edge. It is no scythe. Yet I cut through the enemy's gorget, severing his head at a stroke. The body tumbles away, its jump pack sending it on an uncontrolled flight.

My line is as straight as before. It takes me to the open side door of the Thunderhawk.

There are still three Blood Disciples aboard.

Blurring. Superimposition. Not Blood Disciples. Sons of Horus. The eye of ultimate betrayal emblazoned on the cuirass of their armour.

I descend upon them as they prepare to leap. I collide with one with enough force to knock him across the troop hold and out the open door on the other side. The other two take a fatal moment to react. I swing the Crozius down on the helmet of the Traitor – *Son of Horus/Blood Disciple/all Traitors/any Traitor* – to my right. Crackle and flare of power. Ceramite parts. I sink the head of my weapon deep into his skull. His legs collapse.

Grind of teeth behind me. I duck and whirl. The chainaxe passes over my head. I shoot up. A bolt shell smashes the shaft of the axe. The Traitor brings what is left down on me, using his mass and speed as a weapon. The blow jars me. The temerity outrages me. I yank the Blood Crozius from the head of the fallen Traitor and slam it into the other's chest. His armour resists, but the force of the impact rocks him back on his heels. I hit him again, and again, cracking armour and bone. Red behind my eyes, and red flashing in the gunship's hold. Anger within and anger without. The Crozius is sacred rage incarnate. The spirit of our Chapter (*Legion*) given shape. The icon of faith that is nothing but destruction. The Traitor blocks one of my blows. I fire multiple bolt shells, point-blank, into the broken armour.

I turn from the body just as the Traitor I had hurled from the gunship returns. His landing is awkward. He had to arrest his fall and catch up with the Thunderhawk. I turn his achievement to ash. I meet his stumble with a strike to the shoulder, and the base of his neck. The pauldron shatters. He smashes the side of my helmet with his bolter. My head rings.

red red red redredredred

I hit him again. The Blood Crozius' power is my rage itself. They entwine. The head goes deep. I haul low, forcing him down, severing the tendons to his right arm. He manages to shoot with his left. I feel shells hit my armour. They are irrelevant. I raise the Crozius again. I am yelling, invoking the names of the Emperor and Sanguinius, cursing the Traitors and all their works. I smash my enemy's spine. He still lives, but cannot move. I fire into his jump pack until the promethium sprays in the troop hold, and then once more, igniting the fuel.

I stride through the flames to the cockpit. I tear the door open. The pilot turns his head. I fire my bolt pistol into his helmet until his skull and the treachery within it are splattered across the flight controls and the canopy. The Thunderhawk's nose dips into a steep dive. I throw the corpse aside, take its place, and arrest the fall. I am no pilot, but I know enough to enact my will. Fury is my inspiration. The pain of the Angel's fall calls for the greatest retribution.

I bank the Thunderhawk towards its starboard companion. I unleash the full complement of missiles.

I leave the cockpit and jump from the gunship. I rise above the disaster I have caused. The Thunderhawk I targeted is a ball of flame, still in flight but dropping. It is shooting back at the first. The third gunship has turned towards the fray. It is firing at both. Around and above the Thunderhawks, the air is filled with smaller clashes. Blood Disciples and the Death Company ride the flames of the jump packs. Two rages struggle. Ours is the greater.

In their minds, my brothers fight for the Imperium at its most desperate hour, and they fight with the moment of our greatest wound eternally fresh. They strike with no thought of defence, no thought of survival. The Blood Disciples are here to achieve a purpose. We are here simply to exterminate them. Our martyrs streak into the teeth of enemy fire. Injuries mean nothing. They hammer the foe with bolter fire, and with the impact of their own bodies. Blood Angels and Traitors fall from the sky, locked in mortal struggle. Some rise again, climbing through smoke and fire to seek the advantage of height. The advantage is of more importance to the Blood Disciples. We outnumber them. Our fury surpasses theirs. My brothers are dying, but we are tearing the enemy to pieces.

Two of the enemy Thunderhawks fall to earth. Their fiery ends immolate hundreds of the wrathful, but I do not hear the explosions. They are drowned out by a greater sound behind me. The roar of a terminal wind.

I land in the midst of my scorched earth. I turn to face the roar.

It is blood. A surging, twisting column rises to challenge the height of Hive Profundis. It pierces the cloud cover. The sky tints red. Tiny objects in its vicinity are falling to the ground. Our Thunderhawks.

The pillar of blood resonates with the red of my vision. It stands apart from time. The world shifts, blurs, melts. Eras compete for my belief. I slip deeper and deeper into the Black Rage. I cannot trust belief. But I do not care. I soar on wrath.

Submerge in it.

When am I?

Back and forth, red and black, Terra and Phlegethon. Irrelevant.

Who am I fighting?

Treason.

The solid things: the presence of enemies, my brothers in black, and the blood.

I have a link to the pillar. If I enter it, I am damned. I will not, then. Let it be the monument to all rage.

And let me be all rage.

I do not watch the Thunderhawks hit the ground. The Traitors are closer.

With our first clash, we have stopped their advance. Now on either side we rise to the skies again, converging our strength. I call to my brothers. The Death Company unites to kill the Traitors of all eras.

The dark miracle occurred. The priorities of the mission changed. Corbulo saw the fall of the gunships. He felt the soul-tug of the pillar of blood. He felt a dangerous thirst. The closer he or any Blood Angel came to that vortex, the more dangerous it would be. And he had just seen thirty battle-brothers of Fourth Company, including the captain, brought down.

Just to the east, the Blood Disciples fought the Death Company. The Stormravens engaged the last of the enemy's Thunderhawks. The Traitors had been drawn from the Iron Guard. They were held, and they were being bloodied.

Corbulo dropped into the interior of the *Phlegethon*. 'Sergeant Gamigin,' he said, 'you have seen?'

The sergeant nodded, his eyes haunted. 'Our captain needs us.'

'Agreed. You should speak to the commander of the Iron Guard. The Death Company has its fill of enemies. Best to keep it that way.'

Gamigin understood. He raised Reinecker on the vox. 'Colonel,' he said, 'we are moving to provide assistance closer to the gates. Until we return, it is imperative that you hold your position.'

'You will fight all our battles for us?' the colonel's voice crackled back.

'We intend no such thing. But you must not interfere with the engagement currently under way. Please acknowledge.'

There was a pause. 'Acknowledged.'

Gamigin met Corbulo's gaze. 'Will he listen?'

'May the Emperor grant that he does.'

We are the black. We are the rage. Our formations are loose. Provisional. So are the enemy's. We fight one-on-one, and in groups of three. We ride fire to the skies, each seeking the advantage of height.

The blur.

Nothing but the blur.

Terra, this is...

No...

Yes...

Terra.

Blur.

The enemy, my brothers, the blood, the fury.

Treason. No greater treason. The most trusted of brothers destroying the greatest of dreams.

Meet it with the greatest of rage.

The Angel is with us. I am Sanguinius. The Angel is falling, falling, fallen.

Blood. They have taken the most glorious blood. Tear them apart. Make them pay with blood in unending torrents. Turn the world to blood.

Blood touches the sky. Blood pierces the sky.

The blood is rage.
The blood is everything.
The blood of everything.

The enemy dares to fight. He dares to resist judgement. My brothers roar their outrage.

The vox explodes with anger. Curses in High Gothic. Vengeance promised. The death of Horus is coming.

There are other howls, too, beyond words.

A distant echo wails that we are mad, that nothing but the struggle itself is real. Whose cry is this?

No one's.

Four Traitors converge on me as I descend from a jump. The armour shifts colour schemes. Their identity is fluid (*Disciples Sons Children Alpha Night Iron*) and solid (*Traitors*). I empty my bolt pistol's clip at one as he climbs. I blast through his gorget and turn his throat to a void. He rises past me, his jump pack carrying his corpse on one last arc.

A second grapples with me as I maglock the pistol. We hit the ground like a bomb, our grip on each other unbroken. We crush mortals (*heretics*) beneath us. Their blood splashes up our boots. We trade blows, Blood Crozius against chainsword. I am wounded. I don't know where. The runes on my lenses are smears. I sense only the fact of the outrage as a fuel for rage.

I shatter the chainblade with the Blood Crozius. He stumbles, arms extended. I sever the right one at the elbow. But his two brothers are upon me now. Impact of bolter shell against my right flank. Grind of a combi-bolter's blade against my left.

I snarl, lash out to my right. The Crozius bites through his lenses. And now two of my brothers have joined us.

And more of the enemy.

A gathering of rage. A clenched fist of war.

Blinded by rage, I have no body. I am violence itself. It speaks through my throat. I am preaching to my brothers though I have no thought to the words. I strike and strike and strike. Individual foes vanish. They become a single abstraction. I will rend its flesh. My armour is the white bone on night, it is death, and I am death. A brittle resistance. It is bone. I pull it apart. A soft resistance. Organs and vitae. Ripped apart.

Covered in blood I cannot drink. I taste its smell.

It is more fuel.

My brothers in night, in vengeance. We kill without restraint.

Without reason.

Without end.

Reinecker climbed the wreckage that had been *Guardian of Kulth*. The north, south and west walls of the Iron Guards' position were still under siege by the mob, but holding it off was not difficult now that the pressure from the east had been relieved. He looked that way now. The pillar of blood drew his eyes and repulsed them. There was nothing in his faith or knowledge that could explain it. It was a violation of both. The Emperor's galaxy did not permit such a thing. But it was there, a wound in the world, and to any soul that gazed upon it. He looked at where it disappeared though the clouds. He wondered how much higher it went, and he was scared to know.

'What is that, Preacher Auberlen?' he asked the man who had accompanied him to the *Guardian*.

The Ministorum priest had taken only a short look at the pillar before turning away. He had his back against the Chimera. His lined, sharp features had been, for as long as Reinecker had known him, as inflexible as dogma, as unchanging as bronze. Now they seemed brittle. 'That is not what it appears to be, colonel,' Auberlen said. His voice sounded thin. There was no authority of religious command.

'I am very glad to hear it,' Reinecker said. 'But what *is* it, then?'

'That is not for us to say.'

'It is for you!'

'It is an illusion,' Auberlen said. He gathered his robes as if he were tightening the hold of his faith around his soul. 'If you'll excuse me, colonel, I should see to the spiritual strength of the company.' He clutched his rosarius hard enough that blood dripped from his palm. He walked away.

An illusion? Reinecker thought. He bit back his retort. He wanted to chase after the priest and shake him. He wanted to demand how he planned to perform his duties when he was guilty of such fundamental evasion. He restrained himself. Anger now helped nothing. And the anger came so easily.

The anger. It existed on Phlegethon like the wind. It was more than an emotion, and more than a plague. He didn't know how such a thing was possible, either. And because it wasn't, he told himself that he was mistaken. The temper that he was holding in on a short leash was understandable. It was a result of the reverses his regiment had experienced. That was all.

He turned his face from the pillar. He would avoid the sight of one supreme blasphemy, and deny the existence of others. That, he knew, was the path of his duty.

But the path couldn't stop there. The Blood Angels had ordered him not to interfere with the fight against the Traitor Space Marines. He chafed at the presumption of that command, as if the Iron Guard were serfs of the Adeptus Astartes. He watched the struggle. The Blood Angels fought with a savagery that took him aback. It was out of character from what little experience he had had fighting alongside that Chapter. There was a nobility to the Blood Angels, and a pride, he believed, that was not so far removed from the Iron Guard's own sense of self and honour. But these warriors, in black rather than red, were even more brutal than the enemy. They were predators, tearing the foe to pieces. Some of their roars reached his ears, but he couldn't make out the words. He wasn't entirely sure there were any.

One Blood Angel was central to the fray. He appeared to be in command, though Reinecker didn't know how there could be leadership in that maelstrom of violence. His helmet bore the skull that the colonel knew to be the emblem of a Space Marine Chaplain. But the emblem extended to the rest of the armour. The arms, legs, and torso bore the design of bones as well. Reinecker kept seeing a figure of Death itself loose on the battlefield. A skeleton surrounded by an aura as massive as night.

Movement at his shoulder. Commissar Fasza Stromberg had joined him. She gazed for a moment at the pillar of blood, then turned away from it as resolutely as he had.

'How is morale?' Reinecker asked her.

'Better than it was. Worse than it could be. What are your orders, colonel?'

Mine? Or the ones I've been given? he thought. He took in the full picture of the battlefield. The Blood Angels column was moving to assist the downed gunships near the pillar. The Traitors who had been besieging the regiment were being taken apart by the squads in black, and the fight had moved slightly south of the Mordians' position. Reinecker realised he had a clear run straight to the gates of Hive Profundis.

'We attack,' he said. He would not interfere with the skirmish before him. The regiment would drive past it, smashing through the mob. He still had enough heavy armour to challenge what the Traitors had stationed at the wall. He had no illusions about a full breakthrough into the city, but with the Blood Angels armour that close...

The Adeptus Astartes acting in support of the Astra Militarum. That would be something for morale. That would be something for the history of the regiment. That would be something for glory.

'We attack,' he said again.

The psychic undertow grew stronger as the armoured column drew closer to the pillar of blood. The daemonic wonder was fountain, and it was tower, and it was serpent. Its spin generated a constant wind. The sound was a hollow roar through a Titan's war-horn. It was a call of rage, never spent, eternally building. Its shadow fell over the soul of every Blood Angel. Periodically, it threw out a stream of blood that reached over the plain to fall in a narrow band of crimson rain.

'Do not come into contact with the blood,' Corbulo voxed. He didn't know if that had been the cause of the gunships' fall or not. He thought it might be. The spiritual peril of the pillar was extreme.

The Thunderhawks had come down over a relatively small area. There was that small mercy, Corbulo thought. The pilots had retained that much control. The mercies stopped there. Two of the gunships were in flames. The *Primarch's Wings* was still intact, its nose crumpled by impact. The *Phlegethon* made for it first. The column split up into three, a group of vehicles and squads heading for each crash site. Gamigin had nominal command, but the circumstances were perilous at a level that touched directly to Corbulo's authority. They all felt it. What the Blood Disciples had unleashed was far more dangerous than they were.

Fires had spread over the region of the impacts. There was little vegetation. What burned was the bodies of the wrathful. While they lived, they ran shrieking, and brought the flames to others, a real fire consuming the one that burned inside their hearts and minds. There were corpses everywhere, but even more of the frenzied population rushed to the fallen gunships. The tanks drove over them. The devastator squads marched beside the vehicles and purged the land ahead with heavy bolters and heavy flamers.

As they reached the *Primarch's Wings*, Corbulo saw Castigon and several battle-brothers fighting the mob. His relief was short-lived. Castigon and the others were killing for the sake of killing. There was nothing these people with their crude weapons could do to a Space Marine. The captain was engaged in slaughter. Corbulo saw him grab a mortal by the neck and rip his throat out. A torrent of blood sprayed into Castigon's face, and he drank it down, snarling. He threw the corpse aside, cut another mortal in half with his chainsword, and waded deeper and deeper into the sea of vitae.

The Red Thirst. The other curse, the other madness. Like the Black Rage, it ended only in atrocity. The Rage, though, was the perversion of the nobility of the Chapter. It sprang from the genetic memory of betrayal and the loss of the finest of them all. The

Thirst was the expression of the worst of the Blood Angels' nature. It was the shame. Lemartes and the Death Company inspired horror, pity and grief. But also honour. Grandeur. They embodied heroism and self-sacrifice even when reason had departed.

Corbulo saw only tragedy and waste in what had taken Castigon. He and the others had become savage. Animals.

Corbulo jumped down from the *Phlegethon*. He waded through the mortals, killing them as he walked, but careful to keep his actions cool, impassive. 'Brothers,' he voxed. 'Calm is our greatest weapon. The symbol of our peril towers above us. Restraint is our shield, and the salvation of our afflicted brothers.'

He closed with Castigon while the rest of the squads worked to overpower and subdue the other sufferers of the Thirst. He maglocked his bolt pistol and held his right hand out to the captain. He raised what he had in his left: the Red Grail. It had held Sanguinius' blood. It was the direct link to everything the Blood Angels had once been. It glowed with a red as deep and fierce as the monstrosity that roared and howled at impossible heights. But this was not the blood of hunger. It was the blood of strength. Corbulo vowed to bring all these brothers back from the red oblivion of the Thirst, but the company needed its captain first and foremost. He refused to let Phlegethon strike so hard a blow against them so early in the war.

'Brother-captain,' he said, 'look upon this. This blood of our primarch was gathered for us in this chalice. Know his blessing. He guides us still. He guides you right now. Castigon, do you hear me?'

Castigon held his chainsword. Its blade, like his armour, like his face, was covered in blood. He stood knee-deep in bodies. They were barely recognisable as having been human. They were a mass of organic waste, a muck of viscera from which poked bones, hands and a lower jaw. Castigon was snarling with every breath. His eyes shone with a feral joy. Lost in the ecstasy of bloodlust, he started to lunge at Corbulo, but stopped at the sight of the Red Grail. He hesitated, the teeth of the chainsaw whirring at high speed.

Gamigin and Albinus came up behind him. Corbulo signalled for them to wait.

'*Do you hear me?*' he insisted.

Castigon stared at the Red Grail. He stopped breathing. Time was suspended. The chalice seemed to become heavier in Corbulo's grasp, as if it now held Castigon's soul. 'Let the Angel guide you,' he said to the captain.

Another heartbeat passed in the pool of stillness, surrounded by the carnivore rampage of wrath and war, towered over by the great pillar, the blood that was fuelled by the rage, the blood that fuelled the Thirst.

The suspension ended. Castigon fell to his knees. He breathed once more, and there was sentience in his eyes again. Then there was agony. He gazed at the Red Grail and said, 'Blood of Sanguinius, forgive me.'

'Our father understood, brother-captain,' Corbulo said. 'I am grateful for your return.'

Gamigin helped Castigon to the *Phlegethon*. Corbulo turned to the other Blood Angels caught in the Thirst. As he moved to help, the Grail before him, the volume of weapons fire intensified to the north and west. He looked, expecting to see the rest of the Blood Disciples moving to engage, now that their ritual was complete. But they had not left their position. They had ignored the Blood Angels advance, and they remained in an entirely defensive posture, still protecting their prophet.

Then the vox exploded with the cries. 'No,' Corbulo whispered, as if denial mattered at all.

We hurl the Traitors into the jaws of oblivion. Their every effort at retaliation dooms them to worse slaughter. Every blow they land is a spur to greater rage.

Crimson flash and obsidian cracks, strobe and vibration, intensities meeting in a single unending burst.

The world gone. The walls of the Palace a mere shadow, mist vanishing beneath the redblackredblack.

Only the enemy.

Render him formless.

Turn all into the crimson night.

Wrath mounts from paroxysm to paroxysm. No vengeance will suffice. The crimes are beyond measure. So must be retribution. I cannot kill with enough violence.

Because rage has no peak. There is always more.

Always another level of fury. The tower rises to the infinite.

The pillar of blood, vertical sinuosity, a wound in my vision. Disrupting the perfection of the storm. But embodying the storm.

Energy, conception, abstraction, embodiment.

Rage and fuel of rage.

Hunger.

My universe is the next blow. My soul is my enemy's death. My brothers and I rise in the air. I know we do so. Where or how high is insignificant. The leaps take us to the throat of the foe. I see all that is necessary. The route to the kill.

My brothers are on Terra. They call names dead ten thousand years. They answer to those names. I *am/am not* with them. I have left Phlegethon. The name is a faint memory. Lost to history yet to come. Terra is a smear, a fragile real.

Retribution is all that matters.

The enactment of rage.

I am shouting. I hear some of my words. I hear sounds that are not words. They are the hymn of the wrath. They bind my brothers to me. I hear them in all the levels of reality. The registers of delusion. So they hear me. Sermon, rage and orders are one. The Death Company attacks with the precision of madness.

The enemy vanishes.

Have we killed them all? The Black Rage burns unslaked.

A faint rumble through the huge roar of my blood. Clanking of treads. The hulking of shadows. They gather substance as my fury turns their way. The Traitors are bringing their heavy armour to bear.

Protect the walls! End the siege!

We fall on the Traitors. Their numbers have grown. An endless supply to kill. We deliver justice. We summon blood.

Blood everywhere.

We tear the Traitors' bodies to shreds.

A voice is calling to me. Small, distant. Desperate for my attention. It might be mine. I ignore it.

The Traitors die easily.

So easily.

The 237th was almost level with the conflict when the Traitor Space Marines retreated. What was left of them. The black-clad Blood Angels had hurt them badly. Reinecker guessed fewer than half of the enemy's contingent was returning to base.

He was riding in *Wall of Discipline*, one of four surviving Chimeras. As a mobile command vehicle, it had nothing except armour and a vox. It would do. The entire regiment would do. Only a third of the heavy armour remained. The infantry had been brutalised, but they were Mordians, and they had numbers enough to count.

Still the mob was everywhere. The millions that would never be exhausted until the source of the plague was isolated and purged. Because they *were* facing a plague, Reinecker thought, averting gaze and mind from the pillar of blood. A plague. He would not think of any other possibilities.

Glory would stop the clamour of the dark. Glory would help dim the sight of the pillar. For him, for his troops, for the Imperium, this march was necessary.

Hellhounds to the fore again, burning the wrathful. The mob was thinner here. No need for the Wyverns. Another thousand metres, and his cannons would be in range of the Traitors' base. He would open with a massive barrage. He would widen the column, unleash every Leman Russ and Wyvern he had left.

All this went through Reinecker's mind as he saw the Traitors retreat. The front of the column drew abreast of the Blood Angels squads. The Adeptus Astartes launched upwards once more.

Towards the Mordians.

Reinecker frowned. He couldn't process what he was seeing. The angle of the jump made no sense. Why weren't they pursuing the Traitors?

Why were they shooting?

Bolter shells shrieked past his head on a diagonal path to the infantry. Cries from behind. The sounds of running boots, attempts at evasion, and the spread of confusion as soldiers collided with the mob.

The Blood Angels were still in the air when the grenades hit. Kraks thrown with inhuman exactness. They landed just in front of their targets. Their shaped charges blasted upwards as the tanks rolled over them. The explosions punched through armour and ripped treads from their wheels. The tanks slewed to stops, their hulls colliding. Two grenades hit *Wall of Discipline*. It shook violently, tried to grind itself into the earth. It threw Reinecker out of the hatch. He landed hard, knocking the breath from his lungs. He struggled to his feet before he was trampled.

The Blood Angel with bone iconography armour stood on the roof of the Chimera. He threw a grenade through the hatch, then fired his jump pack for another short boost. He came down on a Leman Russ. He swung his crozius and decapitated the heavy-bolter gunner. He yanked the body free, fired a volley from his bolt pistol into the interior, and then jumped into the infantry. His brothers followed him. They were a wave of darkness. They disabled every vehicle in their path, slaughtered each crew, and moved on. They were fast, unstoppable, and more terrifying by far than the Traitors.

They were monsters.

The voices from their helmet speakers were rasping, hate-filled howls. Reinecker heard words, but he could not understand them. He recognised a few as High Gothic. The words were fragments of bone in a swamp of inarticulate rage. They fell on the infantry and their actions expressed the wrath that words could not. The Mordians defended themselves, but there was no defence against death itself. Las-fire scarred ceramite. A frag grenade landed at the feet of the dark leader. The explosion killed three members of the Iron Guard, and enraged the Blood Angel still further. He swung his crozius like a pendulum, severing spines. He had maglocked his pistol to his thigh, and with his right hand, he punched through skulls, grabbed throats and ripped them out. As he killed, he ranted. He was no more coherent than the others, but there was a consistency of tone to his ravings, and a distinct rhythm. He was roaring a sermon, Reinecker realised. He was judging the Mordians. He was punishing them.

An inexplicable guilt joined Reinecker's horror.

He had landed to the side of the column, out of the way of the advance of the Blood Angels. He pulled away from the blows of the mob, firing into the masses with his laspistol, and ran alongside the killing machines. He called to them. He pleaded with them. And while he pleaded, he did not shoot. If he could make them hear. If he could make them stop.

He failed. They moved down the regiment, and turned the hard ground into a mire of blood. Reinecker surrendered all hope of reasoning with the monsters. He joined his men in futility and ran into the confused throng of his troops. He aimed his laspistol at the Chaplain and pulled the trigger. 'Fire!' he shouted. 'Open fire! Take them down!'

He had no vox. His own voice was drowned out by the battle and the amplified raging of the Blood Angels. No one could hear his orders. No matter. The Mordian Iron Guard was under attack, and it responded. The few tanks that were left trained their guns on Space Marines. Reinecker ducked as he heard the chatter of heavy-bolter fire. One of the Blood Angels was caught in a crossfire of shells from Leman Russ tanks on either side of the column. He stumbled. The tank on the south flank, nearest Reinecker, fired its cannon, heedless of the density of the melee. The shell exploded against the Space Marine. It blew a hole in his armour and punched through his chest, leaving a smoking void. The blast disintegrated the troopers nearest the Blood Angel.

It robbed them of mere seconds of life.

The tanks didn't last much longer. The other Blood Angels took them out before the echoes of the cannon had faded.

Then the monsters showed Reinecker a new dimension of rage.

CHAPTER FIVE

The Voice

They die so easily.

Too easily.

An impression more than a thought. A passing flicker, the beat of an insect's wings, then gone.

Not quite gone. It leaves a flaw in the uniformity of the rage. A hairline crack in the periphery of the vision. I smash two more Traitors to pulp with consecutive blows of the Blood Crozius.

Too easily.

An insistent buzz now. The crack growing longer, a jagged splinter of light. It will not be ignored.

Stop.

The buzzing would restrain me. I shout my outrage and fight harder. The Traitors dissolve before my judgement. They are nothing but weak bags of vitae.

The stench of blood is thick. It coats my armour. It drips from the Crozius and my gauntlets.

Stop.

The buzzing multiplies. A choir of faint discord whispers in my ears. But Horus' forces are still lined before me... *Too small.*

Too weak.

Stop.

Large shapes in the red and black. The Traitors have brought reinforcements. Terra's plight grows. They have us surrounded. I focus on the threat, force clarity through the sheet lightning of the fury. Tanks, more powerful than the ones we have destroyed.

More familiar.

The Traitors are much larger too.

No.

It is these ones who are small.

Stop.

They surround, but they do not attack. They are still. Why don't they attack? I don't understand.

Think. See. Stop.

The Blood Crozius hesitates in mid-swing.

Sharp edges to the shapes. Details appear. Colours. More red, but not the red of the vengeance. What is red is solid, real, an anchor.

Armour.

It is armour. Red armour. The same as mine...

No. The red on my arm is blood. Beneath it, the ceramite is black.

What am I?

The voice growing clear, loud. It will be heard. It will be obeyed.

You are the Guardian. You have a charge. You have abandoned it.

Stop now. In the name of Sanguinius–

'*Stop!*' I thunder.

The command is to myself as well as to my brothers. My vision clears. The red and the black retreat to peripheral shimmer and flickering cracks. I am not on Terra. I am on Phlegethon. And my boots are deep in the blood of loyal soldiers of the Imperium. I am holding a man by an arm. The bones move freely beneath my grip. They are powder. The man, in a colonel's uniform, is sagging, going into shock. I release him, and he falls to his knees. We are surrounded by the battle-brothers of Fourth Company. They have not closed with us, yet. I have been given a chance to end the unleashed madness.

My shout still reverberates. The Death Company hesitates in its massacre of the Iron Guard.

'*Brothers!*' I call. '*The enemy retreats!*' I speak to the truth in the delusion. The phantom of the Imperial Palace hovers before my eyes. I know I am not on Terra, but I feel myself there. I speak in terms that overlap the realities of the Black Rage. '*We have no time for mere serfs! The Angel needs us!*'

My brothers-in-doom release the last of their victims. The ease of the killings makes it possible to redirect the focus of their wrath.

I look to my left, and see where we must go.

'*With me! With Sanguinius!*' With that, I lead a new march. Three Rhinos stand open to receive us. I enter the centre one, *Bloodpyre*. The Death Company follows. I wish I could be in all three. As if anything could ease my brothers' journey.

The Rhinos are specialised. They have the colours of the Death Company. They are the fit transport for useful madmen. We sit on the benches, and adamantium restraints clamp down over our shoulders. We are immobilised. I speak to the Death Company over the vox. 'We journey to further war, brothers. We will pierce the Traitors' hearts with our blades.'

I do not lie. I never shall. Do my words sink into the tortured consciousness of my brothers? Do they give any comfort at all? Any relief from the confusion and anger created by the restraints? I choose to hope that they do. Little as it is. The Lost are raging and struggling to free themselves. The Rhino's hull vibrates with their howls.

My fists are clenched tight around reality once more. I hold it down as the shackles hold me.

The doors close with a bang. We are driven away from the site of our butchery.

We need to retrench. A score of battle-brothers are suffering from the Red Thirst. The Iron Guard have lost all their vehicles and half their infantry. The pillar of blood has changed the face of the conflict. We must find a new strategy. But there is no shelter on the plains. There is Hive Profundis, and then nothing until Hive Corymbus. The few small communities that existed have been razed by the war. So we return to where the Blood Disciples had lain siege to the Mordians. The ground is higher there. The makeshift walls of ruined tanks are useful. Sergeant Gamigin extends the perimeter with Predators and sentries. They hold the mob at bay with fire and chainsword. The Iron Guard salvage enough tents to construct a rough medicae centre for themselves. Our wounded are of a different kind. Corbulo and Albinus help them as best they can in another Rhino.

The Death Company remains in its transports. Its cages. They are placed at the eastern end of the camp. If the enemy attacks, we will be unleashed first. The greatest danger to the base will be the means of its defence.

I do not wait in the Rhinos. I am needed elsewhere before we fight again. But my first stop is the Iron Guard medicae tent.

Silence falls when I step inside. There is no true quiet in this camp, not with the endless baying of the mob. But in this tent, all action ceases. Not a word is spoken. The Death Company is responsible for very few of the injuries here. This is because almost everyone we struck is dead. Even so, everyone here witnessed the disaster. The soldiers do not reach for their weapons. This testifies to the discipline of the Iron Guard. Their instinct must be to defend themselves from me, even though they know this would be futile. They resist the impulse and obey the order not to provoke more slaughter. I respect restraint. I know its struggle.

My weapons are maglocked to my sides. With an effort, I keep my hands open. I will make no fists while in this tent. I walk to the centre. Colonel Reinecker is seated on a stack of empty ammunition cases. His left shoulder and arm are immobilised by dressings. Given the damage I know I did, I suspect they will be amputated.

The colonel is pale, exhausted. Perhaps still in shock. Even so, he stands. We face each other as warriors.

'Colonel Reinecker,' I say, 'I am Chaplain Lemartes. I regret your regiment's losses.'

He doesn't answer at first. I see him wrestling with his anger. He would like to lash out. My words are not soothing. They are not meant to be. They are the truth. They are necessary. Nothing more is.

Few mortals will challenge the Adeptus Astartes. But Reinecker does. 'My regiment deserves an explanation.'

He and the other survivors bear mental wounds. The Iron Guard has been scarred. This is regrettable. It was also avoidable.

'I have spoken with Sergeant Gamigin,' I say. 'You were given specific instructions not to interfere. Had you remained in position, you would not have suffered these losses.'

'We did not interfere.'

'You entered the zone of engagement.' If Reinecker

is going to argue with me about semantics and interpretation, then he is a worse leader than I had guessed.

'I thought...' he says, and hesitates.

'No, colonel. You did not.' He must not try my patience. It is dangerous to seek something that is lost to me forever. But he does not know. The Black Rage is the burden of the Blood Angels. It is also our secret. The witnesses to the event will wonder about it. They will speculate. But they will *know* nothing.

'You humiliated my regiment!'

Pride. The man is brave, but his pride is too great. It makes him foolish. 'No,' I tell him. 'We slaughtered it.' Every trooper in the tent hears me. No, we did not humiliate the Mordians. They may think so, but they are wrong. I *am* humiliating their commanding officer. It is necessary. 'There is no dishonour where there was never a chance. Your soldiers responded as well as they could have. But you led your men. You were hungry for glory. You were warned. The losses are on your head.'

I leave before he has a chance to respond. He hates me as much as he fears me now. I hope he hates himself too. For the sake of his troops.

The survivors of the squads that had moved against the Mordians limped back to the base. At their head, Lhessek marched up to Khevrak. He stopped just short of moving directly into a physical confrontation. 'Where were you?' His helm speaker lengthened his hiss.

Khevrak leaned forward. If Lhessek was going to make an issue of what happened, the dispute would be a short and bloody one. 'Here. Ensuring the Prophet's work is uninterrupted.'

'You saw what happened.'

'Enough. You didn't do well.'

'*We* didn't do well? No, *captain*, we didn't. We lost our air support, and half our brothers. Are we well advanced, *captain*? Was all safe here? Does the war go well?'

Khevrak wasn't wearing his helmet. He kept his face calm for Lhessek's benefit, as calm as features distorted by the runic hatchwork of perpetually reopened wounds could appear. He gave his brother a small smile. Then he slammed the flat of his chainaxe against Lhessek's head and brought his bolt pistol up to his visor. He activated the axe and let it snarl.

Lhessek hadn't drawn his weapons before beginning the confrontation. He grasped his own chainaxe now.

'Be certain,' Khevrak warned.

Lhessek wasn't. But he didn't back down. 'With our tanks, we could have beaten them back.'

'Perhaps.' Khevrak had seen the rout. He had felt the temptation to send in the heavy armour. The defeat had given his rage a bitter taste. But he had held fast. Redemption was close upon them. The perfection of wrath was nigh. But it had not yet come to pass. The Prophet of Blood's work was not complete. Just a little longer yet. 'And if they had managed to divert their heavy armour to that engagement? Or ignored it and marched on this position? What then?'

Lhessek hesitated, chastened by the prospect of the Prophet's second death. 'Then we must strike now,' he said. 'While they are regrouping.'

'You'll have your vengeance,' Khevrak told him. They all would. Over the Blood Angels. Over the Imperium. Over the weakness that called itself reality.

'When?'

Dhassaran had approached. '*Look!*' the Dark Apostle snarled, pointing to the pillar. 'Is your faith so weak, brother? Do you doubt in the face of miracles?'

Lhessek's fist tightened on his chainaxe again, but he did not draw. He turned to Dhassaran. Doing so allowed him to take a step back from Khevrak without losing face.

Khevrak noticed. He had his victory. He lowered his weapons.

'My faith is as strong as yours,' Lhessek said to Dhassaran. 'But I hunger for our enemy's blood.'

'Soon,' Dhassaran said. 'Soon.'

'*Soon!*' the Prophet of Blood roared.

Khevrak looked up, startled. The Prophet couldn't have been responding to Dhassaran. But the conjunction of promise and pronouncement could not be coincidental. The mortal vessel of the Blood God made a gesture so violent, Khevrak heard the pop of his shoulders dislocating. The ground trembled again. The crevasse widened, and the pillar surged in strength.

'We must see,' Dhassaran said.

'Come with us,' Khevrak said to Lhessek. Then, raising his voice, 'All of you who took our anger to the Blood Angels, come with us.'

'This is the reward for your sacrifice,' Dhassaran told them. 'The blood you shed for the Blood God was not in vain. You did not suffer a defeat. You took us another step down the path to our destiny.'

They rode their jump packs up the spires of Hive Profundis. Khevrak, Dhassaran, Lhessek and the twelve survivors of the squads who had fought with him. They climbed in stages, launching from peak to peak. They ascended through smoke. There were still millions inside the city, millions fighting and burning, killing themselves, turning Profundis into a mountain of fire. Khevrak felt an exhilaration he had not experienced since his conversion. Transcendence was approaching. The entire planet would become an avatar of rage. The efforts of the Blood Angels were futile.

They entered the cloud cover, then climbed beyond it. They reached the roof of the apex spire, and they gazed at the pillar of blood. It now dwarfed Profundis. Night was falling once again, and the blood reached up to the stars. At a height that Khevrak judged must be beyond Phlegethon's atmosphere, the blood spread tendrils across the firmament.

'It is grasping the stars,' Lhessek said, his voice filled with wonder at the power of their god.

'Soon it will pull them down,' Dhassaran said.

Soon, Khevrak thought, the voice of the Prophet echoing in his mind.

The tendrils formed coils around glints of light. For a moment, Khevrak thought they really were grasping the stars. Then the light moved. Phlegethon's cloud of moons, he realised. The blood was grasping the moons.

And then the Prophet's voice was not an echo. It was real. A single human voice, given the same power as the great fountain of blood, boomed up from the distant, unseen surface beneath the clouds. It cried a single, ecstatic word.

'*Fall!*'

I join Corbulo and Castigon at the rear of the *Phlegethon*. The sergeants of the Knights of Baal are there too. I watch the captain. He has recovered from the Red Thirst, though there has been a cost. A tautness around the eyes. An erosion to the nobility of his bearing. One of our curses has tasted his soul. He knows it hungers to devour him. He is now warier of himself. That is good.

I am mindful of other costs. They may not be present. But this world is testing us. I expect the worst.

The Lord Adjudicator's speech is punctuated by bursts of flame from the *Phlegethon*'s cannon. The burning and butchery of the mob continues without cease. We are not engaged against the enemy, and we are. We plan for the next stage of the campaign while in the midst of killing. The wrath of the world is unceasing. The blood flows and flows and flows.

Hunger. Thirst. Rage. They are the air we breathe. They are toxins that our multi-lungs cannot defend against.

'The danger of that daemonic manifestation is clear to us all,' Castigon says. He gestures in the direction of the pillar of blood. He does not look at it. 'Approaching it is fatal. The closer we are, the more we must concentrate on resisting it. This degrades our ability to wage war against the Blood Disciples. Yet we cannot reach their position without passing in close proximity to the pillar.'

'Long-range bombardment?' Gamigin asks.

'A partial solution. It is unlikely to be enough to force the Traitors out.'

'Even if it could, given enough time,' Corbulo says, 'does anyone here believe time is on our side?'

We do not. The Blood Disciples are not simply waiting for us. What we have seen of their force is almost entirely assault-based. If they have chosen a defensive posture, their reasons for doing so must be powerful.

'So,' Gamigin says, 'we cannot attack without succumbing to madness, yet we have no choice but to attack?'

I do not laugh. Even so small a loss of control is dangerous. My throat grinds at Gamigin's remark. The irony of the situation is clear. As is our path. 'Then the mad must lead the charge,' I say.

Castigon nods. Corbulo is more cautious. He asks, 'You are not affected by the manifestation?'

'We are.'

'Is it responsible for what happened to the Iron Guard?'

'Colonel Reinecker is responsible. The blood has an effect, certainly. But we who suffer the Black Rage are immune to the Red Thirst.'

'That distinction is lost on Reinecker and his troops,' Castigon says.

'But it is real. We see the enemy. We fight to a purpose. With honour.' I hear pride in my voice. I feel no shame. Even as I speak, I know I must avenge the Angel. His fall is a fresh, bleeding wound. I am tired of talking.

The blurring begins again. I clamp down on it.

'Is your frenzy so different?' Castigon asks. His pride is injured.

'It is.' *What motivates Thirst?* I could ask. *What motivates Rage? Do you see the difference? The distinction between instinct and passion?*

He waves away the debate. 'Then we are decided. The Death Company will make the initial assault. The foremost goal must be to kill the Traitors' prophet. We cannot be assured that his death will end the phenomenon that has been unleashed, but if he is the locus of the forces aiding the Blood Disciples, he must be neutralised. At minimum, the enemy's defences must be weakened so the rest of the Company can punch through despite the effect of the pillar.' A blast from the *Phlegethon* forces him to pause. Now he does look towards the hive and the serpentine blood before it. 'Hive Profundis awaits her liberators,' he says.

The briefing concludes. The sergeants leave to rejoin their squads. I head towards the Rhinos that hold the Death Company. Corbulo walks with me. 'You know that Castigon was struck by the Red Thirst,' he says.

'I do.'

'You should also know that I was able to pull him back from its grip.' He clearly expects me to see this as a sign of hope.

'The two curses are not comparable in those terms,' I say.

'I think they can be. Especially given the progress you and I have made today.'

'What progress?'

He looks at me, frowning. 'You don't remember?'

'No.'

'I spoke to you. When you were killing the Mordians. I called your name. You heard my voice and followed it back to the light of reason.'

I heard my voice. Not Corbulo's. 'Your voice did not reach me.'

'Are you sure? Not even in an altered form?'

I have no definitive answer to that.

'Something called you out of the night of rage.'

True. His voice or my will? A combination? If Corbulo is even partially correct, is that not cause for hope? A sign that he may yet find the key to our salvation?

Perhaps my scepticism is caused by an unwillingness to need the help of any brother. My will and my faith have kept me from the final abyss of the Black Rage this long.

'Something did,' I say. My agreement is vague. Corbulo hears what he wants. I mean the opposite.

I do not believe him.

But the thought of a cure seeks to take hold in my spirit. It wants to spread hope. I smother it. I cannot afford such weakness. Even *wanting* to believe Corbulo is dangerous.

We arrive at the Rhinos. We can hear the ranting of my brothers coming from inside. Muffled prayers, chants, threats, roars. Corbulo listens for a moment, then looks over the barricade, beyond the mob on the plain, to Hive Profundis and the pillar. 'If that obscenity forces you under,' he says, 'you may never come out again.'

'I never have,' I remind him. 'The Rage grips me now.' With every second passed, every breath drawn, every syllable spoken, I struggle to stay at the surface of the black ocean.

Flickering red. The reality of Terra forcing itself forward.

'You understand me,' says Corbulo. 'If the worst happens, you will be beyond help.'

I am beyond help now. 'The worst is not the madness,' I say. 'The worst is defeat. The blood cannot stop us from fighting. Your help is more needed here.'

A shadow falls over his features. 'I will do what I can for the captain,' he says.

I indicate the mob. Always baying, always struggling to reach us, always dying. 'The danger is great for him and any of the others who suffered the Thirst.'

'I know. The killing never stops. There is blood in the air. You know me, Lemartes. You know I am vigilant.'

I have done him an injustice. 'You are,' I say.

I turn to the battle-brothers standing sentry before the Rhinos. I am about to order them to open the rear hatches. Before I can speak, there is a rumble of earth thunder. The column of blood grows wider. It shoots for the sky with greater intensity. Corbulo winces. A pressure wave sweeps through my skull. It softens the real. I am standing on an illusion.

The enemy seeks to confound me.

Horus disguises Terra. But I can see the shape of the Imperial Palace. The enemy will rue his sad trickery. He...

No.

The ground steadies. I tighten my grasp on the here and now. Let the past give strength to my rage, I pray. But let the present give it direction.

Howls from inside the Rhinos. A pounding of fists against walls. The torment of my brothers defies understanding. We must grant them the gift of battle. It offers no relief. Only the satisfaction of destroying the tormentors. That is sufficient.

The rage emanating from the pillar continues to hit like waves, flung out by the manifestation's sinuous twists. I am moving deep beneath the sea as I make my preparations. I enter the Rhinos. I speak to each group of brothers. I exhort them, and I pray with them. They hear me. Some understand me. I do not calm them. Nothing can ever do that again. But their raging acquires a focus.

We can give each other nothing but destruction.

It is time. The drivers arrive. They will take us partway across the plain, and unleash the Death Company. I enter the centre Rhino, take my seat and accept my shackles. The hatch slams shut. The light inside the vehicle is dim. The snarl of the engines begins, blending with the snarls of the Lost.

Darkness seeks to creep in at the edges of my vision. Red pulses in the twilight of the compartment. Rage is all. I will take it to Horus...

No.

... to the Blood Disciples. I am prepared to vanish into the war on Terra forever.

The Rhino moves forward.

'*Fall!*'

The voice fills my head. It fills the space of the troop hold. It fills everything. It rends everything. I shake my head, trying to dislodge it. I do not know if I hallucinated the cry or not. The Death Company's shouts stop for a moment, then redouble in strength. My brothers heard what I did. That does not mean it was real.

The Rhino lurches to a stop.

The hatch opens again. The glare of the encampment's lumen poles pierces our gloom. My shackles retract. I stride out of the Rhino. Something is wrong. The voice was no delusion.

Corbulo waits for me. 'We are too late,' he says. 'The enemy has struck first.' He points up.

Red streaks in the black of night. It takes me a moment to realise that what I see is real and not the Rage eating at my vision. There is fire beyond the clouds. Something is coming. From horizon to horizon, the glow and pulse and slash of a legion of descents.

When the streaks pierce the cloud cover, there is only a brief moment between realisation and disaster. My consciousness struggles to encompass the scale of the attack. The sky turns to fire and rock. A swarm of meteors descends upon us. Masses of all sizes rain down. Some will burn up before they hit the ground. Some are as big as gunships. Near the horizon, I see a plummeting mountain.

Then the meteor storm strikes the surface of Phlegethon.

All is flame.

And the voice.

CHAPTER SIX

Firmament's End

The Blood Disciples descended from the heights of Hive Profundis. The sky came down with them. On all sides, fire rained through the clouds. Khevrak moved through a sequence of wonders, a tapestry of a world condemned to wrath. Joy was something he had experienced before. Even as one of the Emperor's Wolves, his existence had been determined by the solemn necessities of war. Perhaps the mortal he had been before his elevation to the Adeptus Astartes had been acquainted with the emotion. That being was dead twice over, and long forgotten. As a Blood Disciple, his soul knew only the multi-hued palette of rage. And yet, as he witnessed the coming to fruition of a great work, an ecstasy took him. If it was joy, it was joy of blood and jagged teeth. It was exhilaration in the face of the full possibilities of wrath.

For the first time since the moment of conversion, the exterior world and his inner experience were in perfect accord. A harmony of annihilation.

Above the clouds, it was the stars themselves that dropped with the Blood Disciples. Points of light in the void moved, swarmed, and became wounds of fire. Within the cloud cover, the spectacle lost detail. It became abstract, a smear of sound and light. Flashes of red. Thunder from above and below. The flame-slash of the near miss. The pulse and drum of ongoing destruction, whose revelation was promised even as it was withheld. Burning light in the darkness, answered by the conflagrations of the hive. Smoke and clouds indistinguishable. A limbo that evoked the ruin of existence.

'Do you see it?' he voxed the others. 'Do you see the glory?'

No answer was needed, but he received it all the same. The shouts of warriors fed by the conjunction of chaos and victory.

Below the clouds, the promised revelation was the landscape of the sublime. Explosions building on explosions, the streaks clear once more, beams of fire that shot from the clouds to the ground. The plain kept disappearing in the flashes of impacts. The thunder was louder than ever. Even though his helmet's auto-senses adjusted to dampen the worst of the noise, the hammering of the planet shook Khevrak's skull. A small meteorite struck the hive less than a thousand metres from his position. It hit with the force of a Deathstrike missile. Midway between the surface and the clouds, Profundis screamed. The fireball blossomed for hundreds of metres. Entire districts vaporised. The structural integrity of most of the upper reaches collapsed. Towers dropped like felled trees. Their mass shattered the habs below. The chain reaction built. An avalanche of millions of tonnes of rockcrete followed the Blood Disciples down. Khevrak yelled in triumph. Mountains were falling in their wake.

And rising over the thunder of impacts, of shock waves and of pulverising rockcrete was the voice of the Prophet of Blood. This was a wonder of its own. The great sermon was no longer just for the ears of the Blood Disciples. Now the truth of wrath had come to all. The Prophet's praise of Khorne entwined with the meteor storm. The words and the devastation mirrored each other. They became each other. Words set the land on fire and hurled bedrock turned to dust at the sky. Meteorites taught the gospel of the Blood God.

'*Behold the hand of rage!*' the Prophet called. '*Behold the works and the lesson! Prepare for the arrival!*'

Khevrak landed in front of the Prophet's hill of rubble. He turned around, savouring the panoply of holocaust. At the last, he gazed up at the Prophet himself, and here was still another wonder. The mortal was transfigured. He was barely recognisable as human. His skin was torn by a thousand cuts. It hung in tattered flaps. Much of it had fallen away and lay discarded at the Prophet's feet. The muscle beneath had grown chitinous barbs and scales. Where his shape was not bleeding flesh, it was rigid, sharp.

His body was cutting itself to shreds from the inside. Blood cascaded down the ruins. It flowed in torrents from the Prophet, and its loss only gave him strength. The bones of his arms and legs had snapped, again and again, until he was a thing of many joints. Though shards of bone poked through the transformed muscle, he showed no sign of falling. His dance was more subtle, more savage, more perfectly twinned to the swaying of the pillar.

His lower jaw was dislocated. It dropped almost as far as his chest. The muscles had stretched, torn, and knotted themselves into a tangle of hooks, and they opened and closed the Prophet's maw. His lips had grown into torn curtains. His tongue uncoiled a full metre from the jaws. There was a scorpion's stinger on the end. It stabbed at the Prophet's chest, at his throat, at his eyes. He injected himself with his own venom at every beat of his litany.

The Prophet should not live. He should not speak. But he was the conduit of a force beyond measure. The rage of Phlegethon fed on itself, stung itself, bled itself, and so climbed to ever more transcendent levels.

Arrival, Khevrak thought. All the miracles thus far were still a prologue. A being was coming. *Arrival.* That would be the moment of transfiguration and redemption. He hoped there would still be Blood Angels left alive to witness the full measure of their defeat.

The blood called the moons of Phlegethon. The phantasmal force of the pillar of blood, pulled from the warp, powerful with the irrational, impossible potential of the immaterium, reached into the cloud. Given purchase in the material realm, it devoured the real, and grew stronger as it spread its infection. The more it destroyed of the real, and the more it propagated the unreal, the more its power grew, and the greater the scale of its wonders became. It destroyed the fragile gravitational equilibrium that kept the moons in such close orbit. The cloud of rocky bodies contracted around the parent world. The orbits decayed. The moons fell in their thousands. Many burned up before they reached the surface. Many more did not. The storm hit the entire planet at once. The southern land mass had been spared the plague of wrath. Now wrath came in another form, and the war was truly global.

A moon several kilometres wide hit the ocean south of the equator, within sight of the coastal city of Penitence. The city did not tower like Profundis. It spread its hundreds of millions over a region a thousand kilometres on a side. The blast hit with a wind of seven thousand kilometres per hour. It levelled all the spires. Ten million inhabitants died in an instant. Those who survived, in stronger habs or in the underhive, lived a few more minutes. The wave arrived. A hundred metres high, it brought the ocean with it. It swept over Penitence, scouring it from the earth, reaching deep into the city's roots to drown all who hid and trembled there.

Built on the slopes of the Cinis Mountains, Hive Dacrima did not suffer the same fate as Penitence. It was hit by numerous smaller bodies. Its wall collapsed. Craters appeared where thousands had lived. Firestorms swept from impact site to impact site. Dacrima was besieged by the sky, and though its citizens wept and prayed, there was no surrender to be made. There was only death, and loss, and the wailing of the bereaved.

Phlegethon groaned under a planet-wide artillery barrage. In the first few minutes of cataclysm, hundreds of millions died. The world's tragedy was that billions survived. They saw the end of everything they knew. They saw their cities and homes and cathedrals toppled. They experienced the destruction of any form of certainty.

And they heard the voice.

The Prophet of Blood's sermon reached every living soul on Phlegethon. It had no source, yet it was as real as the winds. It was the voice of the disaster itself. It was the end of a faith that had failed when it was most needed.

'Where is your false god?' the Prophet demanded. *'Where is he in the darkness? Where is he in the flames? You have kept faith, and you have been abandoned.*

How will you answer the false god? How will you avenge your betrayal?'

The people answered with rage. They cursed the Emperor who had turned His back on them. Their rage grew. Those who had lost everything looked on those who had retained something. Those who had lost less regarded those who had nothing with fear. In the vicinity of Hive Profundis, the mob had targets for its hate. Elsewhere, there was no one except other citizens. They turned on each other. Billions fought with billions as the sky continued to fall.

Rage swept over the world. It was a psychic wave more destructive than anything unleashed by the falling moons.

There is no shelter.

Impacts shake the plains. Thousands of mortals die every second, disintegrated by impacts, smashed by the blast waves, incinerated in fireballs.

'Stand fast, brothers,' Castigon orders over the vox. We do. There is nowhere to turn. The bombardment will hit us, or it will not.

There is an impact not far to the north of our position. My lenses shutter themselves against the glare of the blast. They open again as the wind hits us. It tosses the wreckage of our walls. It tries to lift me off my feet. I sink to one knee and punch my fists deep into the ground. Beside me, Corbulo does the same. We are anchored. Some distance to my left, the Mordian tents fly off into the booming night. So do soldiers. The remains of a Taurox flip end over end. The wind carries it out of the camp and sends it rolling across the shrieking mob.

When I stand, Castigon already has new orders. 'We make for the crater,' he says.

There are no good choices. The captain has made the best one possible. We will treat the meteorite storm as an artillery attack. The shells are large. Their craters can serve as imperfect shelter.

The nearest lip of the crater is less than a hundred metres away. There is no time or reason to move into formations. We need speed. The vehicles that had been plugging the holes in the northern defences move first, pushing through what is left of the wreckage wall. They open the way for the evacuation. They keep going. The Death Company Rhinos fire their engines and move off in the next wave. Corbulo and I follow on foot. Most of our battle-brothers and the Iron Guard are with us. The south-facing tanks are the last to abandon the encampment.

We leave the gunships. They cannot fly in these conditions. They will remain where they are. May the will of the Emperor shield them. Brother Orias and two other pilots are now at the controls of the Rhinos. When he passed me on his way to the central vehicle, Orias said, 'If I cannot fly, I want my journey across the land to be an interesting one.'

I think his wish will be granted.

The journey is a short one. We are harried by the words of the Prophet of Blood. His sermon attacks and taunts. It rings in our ears, an insistent reminder of the strength of the Ruinous Powers. I refuse to grant him power over my soul. But my hatred of his pronouncements is rage. It is dangerous. I clamp down hard, and try to tune out the Prophet.

Minutes have passed since the first strikes began, and our forces descend into the crater. Castigon has the heavy armour form lines close to the walls of the depression. The shelter is doubtful. It is based more on odds than physical protection. Its benefit is psychological. The Mordians are stoic, but I see relief on their faces. They are human. They are afraid, though they conceal the emotion well.

The storm continues. If a large mass hits, our war will end in an instant. I do not think it will. The annihilation of Profundis and its environs would not serve the purpose of our enemy.

I join Castigon and Corbulo at the eastern lip of the crater. We look across the plain. The rain of stone is heavy between us and our goal. The plain is pockmarked by the fall of many small bodies. An advance through that screen of destruction would be difficult. Perhaps impossible.

'The fall is controlled, isn't it?' Castigon says.

'Yes.' The concentrations of the falls are strategic. The destruction is continuous. The wrathful of Phlegethon die in vast numbers. Our advance is stymied. But there are much larger moons in orbit. None come down here because that would not be useful.

'We must make the attempt,' I say.

A chunk of rock the size of a human skull strikes less than a dozen metres away. It would have reduced a Land Raider to slag.

'At what cost?' Castigon asks. He gestures at the new, small crater. 'What will be left of our company if we are hit by that every step of the way?' He is not reluctant to fight. He is reluctant to engage in futility.

'Only chance has preserved us this far.'

As I finish speaking, the site we abandoned explodes. The ground shakes hard. Stones fall down the walls of our crater. Mortal soldiers are knocked off their feet.

The odds of success have nothing to do with the necessity to act. Castigon is correct. Fourth Company would not reach the Blood Disciples intact. It very likely would not reach them at all. 'The Death Company only,' I say. 'As we discussed. We will attack.' Three Rhinos, moving fast. There is a chance. And we cannot wait for the storm to pass.

Something is coming. I hear its footsteps behind the beat of the meteorite impacts. I hear them in the promises and welcomes of the Prophet of Blood. If we wait, the Blood Disciples will complete their ritual. All that has happened is a means to an end. We must prevent that end from manifesting.

More impacts. More thunder. More trembling of the earth. A small hit takes out a chunk of the western end of the crater. The voice of The Prophet batters the night.

'Staying is no better,' I say.

Castigon faces Profundis.

'There are other craters,' he says.

The landscape of the plain is a pockmarked slaughterhouse. There are several depressions the size of the one we are in now. Fourth Company could choose any. Or all.

'We can make our way forward from crater to crater,' Castigon says. 'It's a small chance. No worse than the one we have now.'

'But how far forward?' Corbulo asks.

The pillar is the barrier. The manifestation must be ended before a full attack is possible. We do not know if the death of the Prophet will be sufficient to that end. It is the only move we have. So we will take it.

'As close as possible,' Castigon says. 'Close enough to bring our guns to bear with full effect.'

And meanwhile the Death Company will use speed. We cannot be held back any longer. Death and fire surround us. My Rage is slipping its leash. Speaking to Castigon and standing still while war erupts strains my will. My fingers vibrate with tension. 'We go now.'

He nods. A strange look in his eyes. He has succumbed once to the Red Thirst. No doubt he mistrusts himself. Perhaps he has begun to question the fitness of his command.

'Lead well, captain,' I tell him. I think he will. Castigon has always been proud. The shock of humility may be a boon to him.

I step towards the Rhinos.

The Prophet shouts, '*We are one in wrath!*'

A presentiment of danger. I reach out for an imagined support. Rage the size of the planet hits us.

Castigon gasps. So does Corbulo. The wave is monstrous.

I need an anchor for this greater wind. There is none. I snarl. My fury blinds me.

Red, blood and fireball, consuming, enveloping.

Only the red.

And the black. Gripping. Adamantium band around my mind.

Not now.

No.

N...

CHAPTER SEVEN

The Dark Ocean

Denial fails me. Phlegethon vanishes at once.

I am on Terra. The Imperial Palace burns to the east.

No, it does not. It is Hive Profundis that burns. I know this. I cannot see it. The reality of Terra is firm. I cannot pierce the lie.

A figure blocks my path. In the burning fog of red and black, I cannot see the colour of his armour. If he seeks to interfere, he is an enemy. I raise the Blood Crozius.

'Chaplain Lemartes,' the shape says. 'Brother.'

He knows me.

I know him. Corbulo.

Phlegethon. I am on Phlegethon.

But all I see, tinted crimson, is Terra.

Thunder. Flashes. Shaking beneath my feet.

Impacts. There is shelter here.

I cannot see the crater. The impacts are from the enemy's cannons. Mounted on the stolen walls of the Palace.

No. That is the lie. Surface from the rage.

'What do you see?' Corbulo asks.

Sinking. Sinking.

'I see you,' I croak. 'Corbulo.'

'Where are you?'

'Before Hive Profundis.' I lie. I cannot be shackled now. I must lead the attack.

I walk forward. I stop. I try again to force the vision away. It shifts, as if broken up by the meteor storm. I am not on Terra. I am on Horus' battle-barge. Decking beneath my feet. Dark walls on either side. Vaults.

Lies. Lies. Lies.

'Where are you?' Corbulo insists. His shape gathers definition. A great eye on his armour.

No. No. No.

'Phlegethon,' I say. I think I do. My lips move. I cannot hear what I say for the clash of guns and the roars of battling Space Marines near me.

That must be a lie too.

But I do not know.

All trace of the real is gone. All I can grasp is the shifting of the illusion. The knowledge that what I see is not real. If I lose that conviction, I am lost.

More words from the Traitor–

Corbulo.

–from Corbulo. I cannot hear them. I do not respond.

I do not move. He repeats himself. 'Where are you going?'

Where?

Down this corridor?

No. No corridors.

The thirst for vengeance saves me. I was going to lead the attack. Truth and delusion intersect for an instant. I remember the goal of the attack. I remember the means. Where am I going? 'To board the Rhino,' I say.

'Where is it?'

I was walking towards it.

Towards what?

Towards the bridge. I will find Horus there. Sounds of battle ahead. The promise of justice.

No.

No. I try to see through the presence of the ship. I cannot. But there were Rhinos near me. On that planet, millennia from here. 'Straight ahead,' I say. I point at a bulkhead.

Out of my way.

The battle clash growing louder. I am needed. I will prevent the Fall.

Out of my way.

'It is not.' The figure before me is an enemy. But he does not attack. He stands still. My hand is closed over the haft of the Blood Crozius, but I do not raise it. *Corbulo,* I tell myself. A name from a memory of the future. *This is Corbulo.*

I hold myself frozen. I cannot believe in what I see.

My cause is clear. My rage has focus. But the means of vengeance are slipping away. I grasp at the single immediate task: *board the Rhino.* The task I cannot complete.

Motionless. Any step could be the wrong one. The Rage plunges me deeper into its lies. The false real of the ship solidifies. It surrounds me with the presence of enemies. My strength is consumed in maintaining awareness of the lie. A slip, and the Rage will control my actions. I will attack.

'Do you hear me, Chaplain Lemartes?' Corbulo asks.

'I do.' Teeth clenched, jaw fused to iron. Speech is a trial.

'Do you see me?'

The shape before me. The shape of my enemy. He–

'No,' I say. Dissembling is pointless.

'Then use my voice. Follow it out of the darkness. You are among brothers. You are not alone.'

He is wrong. The bond of the curse is a fallacy. We share the Flaw. We share the pull of the Red Thirst. But the Black Rage takes its victims behind a wall. Those on the other side of the barrier imagine the journey. They cannot know it. The further down we go, the more isolated we become. Even in the Death Company, the awareness of fellow sufferers is limited. At best. I have been a bridge. I speak from the other side of the wall. I speak to both sides. Corbulo listens, but he cannot truly hear. The Lost of the Death Company do hear. I have created fellowship there. But if I fall, that will be swept away too.

I am falling.

'Take hold of my voice,' Corbulo insists.

The world pounds with impacts. Meteorite strikes. I remind myself of the truth. Not the slamming of torpedoes against the hull. Then another sound. A snarling rumble. Clanking of metal.

Vehicles.

There is no analogue for this sound in the ship. The delusion shatters into black fragments. It reassembles itself as Terra once more. I am hearing the roar of tank engines. I see their shapes in the red-black fog. Details form from the madness. Vehicles unseen for ten thousand years.

No.

In a few moments, they will become the engines of the enemy, and call my wrath to them.

No.

Refuse that lie. They must be our own tanks. Castigon has sent Fourth Company forward.

Has he?

How long have I been standing here?

Can I trust my deduction? I am falling through a choice of delusions.

And Corbulo is still there, still speaking, still throwing me the hope that is his, not mine. I have tried to use his voice as a guide. The effort is futile.

'This is Phlegethon. We march on Hive Profundis.'

'I. Know.' Words ground like glass. Knowledge is

futile in the face of belief. Facts are being crushed by the weight of illusion.

Pointless. Corbulo's efforts are pointless. The uselessness enrages me further. This is not the time to experiment. I have no patience for false hope. His voice grates against my soul. It distracts me from the struggle. Truth grows thin and slippery.

Be quiet. Be quiet. Let me concentrate.

Corbulo's words do not help. They hinder. They work against me. Enemies. Their speaker is my foe.

No. No. No.

I do not attack. I do that much.

But the wrath grows. Black flames consume me. Black waves submerge me.

Plunging deeper into the Black Rage.

Reason fading, breaking. The surface is too far.

Down.

Down.

The Blood Angels moved out of the crater. Armoured vehicles and armoured giants headed into the storm. Reinecker watched. He debated what destruction he should choose for his troops.

He had arrived on Phlegethon at the head of a siege regiment. Now he commanded a diminished infantry. All vehicles gone. The campaign nothing but a series of humiliating defeats. He was just as diminished. His left arm was shattered. His uniform was torn. He would have had nothing but contempt for a Mordian officer who presented so sorry a spectacle.

The Blood Angels captain had not bothered to let Reinecker know what he was planning. The strategy was clear enough, but Castigon had dropped any pretence that the Iron Guard mattered to the war any longer.

'What are your orders, colonel?' Stromberg asked. She had to shout.

The question was loaded. It was a goad. She was less interested in the specific orders than in determining whether he had any to give. Reinecker glanced at her before looking back at the Blood Angels deployment. She was standing with her arms straight. Her bolt pistol's holster was still fastened shut. *So you aren't quite ready to relieve me of command,* Reinecker thought.

What were his orders? To march and die? What other possibilities were there? He could see none. And there was little honour to be found in that course. The Mordians would serve no purpose. They would advance behind the Space Marines, and if any of them survived the gauntlet hurling down from the skies, they would turn their lasweapons on the enemy, accomplish nothing, and be annihilated.

'Colonel?' Stromberg prompted.

'A moment, commissar.'

There had to be another choice. There had to be a meaningful action.

He wrestled with a non-existent dilemma. He knew he was wasting time. It was hard to think. The endless raving of the heretic preacher attacked him from every direction, as if the very air of Phlegethon had become a planetary vox-transmitter. The pressure at his temples mounted. Over the course of the last few minutes, his anger had been growing. The spike had been sudden. Frustration had turned into the need to lash out. And there was no target. Even the mob, that degraded foe, was barely worth the expenditure of ammunition. The people of Profundis were being smashed to dust by the falling sky.

Straight ahead, he saw the target of his fear and resentment. Not all the Blood Angels had mobilised. Three of their armoured transports had not moved. The ones housing the madmen. Their leader, Lemartes, stood a few metres from them. He was motionless. Corbulo was with him, and appeared to be pleading with him.

The pressure in Reinecker's head became a throbbing, tightening band. The thought came to him that the number of soldiers remaining to him could be enough to overcome a single Space Marine.

'Colonel?' Stromberg asked again.

Reinecker gasped. His flesh prickled, suddenly cold. He had just contemplated an act of treason against the Adeptus Astartes. He fought to keep his breathing even. He couldn't let Stromberg guess what he had been thinking. The throb grew even worse. He was furious with himself, with Stromberg for her scrutiny, with Lemartes for what he and his brethren had done to the Iron Guard, and with whatever was leading him to thoughts of treachery.

Reinecker took a breath. 'We march,' he said.

'We follow the Blood Angels.'

'Yes.' His right eye ached, as if a blade of anger was stabbing it from the inside.

'And?'

'And what, commissar?' He rounded on her. Why was she engaging him in pointless discussion? The endless thunder of explosions made it hard enough to think, let alone make himself heard.

'And what do we hope to achieve?' She managed to make her shout icy. She was angry too.

'We achieve following orders,' Reinecker snarled. 'We achieve being true to our duty to the end. We achieve marching like Mordians. Or is that not good enough for you?'

Fine words. He should believe them. Instead, he cursed every syllable he uttered. He hated their truth.

Stromberg's fingers twitched. Reinecker hoped she would reach for her pistol. He didn't know if he would embrace the execution or if he would draw his own sidearm. The intensity of his anger was such that he would welcome its end through death, or its embodiment in violence.

Stromberg grimaced, struggling with her own fury. 'Then give your orders, colonel,' she said. '*Now.*'

He kept staring. He was ready for a battle of wraths. But she said nothing else. He drew his sword. He faced east, raised the blade high, then slashed down and forward. He began to walk, staying close to the crater wall. The infantry followed.

He did not look back. He did not want to see the

ruin that had been his regiment. His anger flashed in the direction of his troops. If they had been so badly defeated, that was a failure. They had failed. They deserved his condemnation.

His throat worked as he swallowed. It felt like a solid piece of his anger was going down his throat, trying to choke him. In its wake came a flash of shame. He did look back now. Wounded, demoralised, knowing as well as he did that they could all be dead in the next few minutes, they marched with the same precision as ever.

Their faces cold with anger.

For a moment, his own anger gave way to pride. And then to revelation. His chest expanded. He was privy to a great truth, though he didn't know what it was. He was seized by a stern joy. There was no reason for it that he could define. He had experienced it in the past, at the end of hard campaigns. At the moment of victory. There was no victory here. He did not understand how he could react as if there was. His only achievement of the last few minutes had been to avoid engaging in pointless, immoral fights.

He wondered if he had sunk so low that he sought gratification in the trivial.

The moment ended. The joy passed. The triumph died. Even so, he felt he had experienced something important. There was a lesson to be drawn, and it was vital he learn what it was.

He drew level with the two Blood Angels. Lemartes had not moved at all. He was motionless as stone, yet he radiated a tension so ferocious that Reinecker's chest tightened again in response.

He looked away from the Chaplain and climbed the slope of the crater wall. At the top, he stared ahead into the hell of explosions and the fire falling from the heavens. The Blood Angels were moving into the next sizeable crater. It was smaller than the first. It would not hold the full company, but there was another beyond it that would be the next target.

No strikes in the same location? Reinecker thought. *Is that the basis of Imperial strategy now?* His anger was back. With it came despair.

And then perfect mockery.

A meteorite hit the bowl of the crater behind him. Reinecker felt the flash. Then he was flying.

The ground disintegrated. The shockwave was the limb of a Titan smashing against Corbulo. It threw him from the crater. For a few seconds, he was in a limbo of tumbling perspective, flying rock, and battering sound. He hit the ground hard. The limbo was still with him. He stood, shaking off the stun, trying to orient himself in the cloud of falling debris, smoke and swirling dust. After a minute, it cleared enough for him to see that he had landed not far from the encampment. 'Lemartes,' he called. No answer on the vox. Only static. He tried contacting Castigon without success. He could still hear the engines of the tanks. His vox-bead must have been damaged in the strike.

He was out of contact with Lemartes. The psychic wave had pushed the Chaplain so far into delusion that there was a risk he could never return to rationality. Corbulo knew Lemartes had no faith in his methods for bringing him back, but there *had* been engagement. Lemartes knew who Corbulo was, and answered when addressed. That was still more than could be said for any other member of the Death Company.

And now Corbulo could not reach him. Lost in his hallucinations, what would he do if he freed his brothers from the Rhinos? They would see anyone they encountered as foe. Corbulo pictured the squads of the Death Company coming up behind the Blood Angels. The fratricidal consequences chilled him.

Corbulo moved through the dust cloud, calling for Lemartes. He held his bolt pistol. He prayed to Sanguinius that he would not have to pull the trigger.

Where am I?

On Terra. Yes, before the Imperial Palace.

The hit from the enemy artillery was a hard one. It knocked me far from where I had been standing.

Standing where? With whom?

The questions are a disturbing irritant. I push them aside.

I do not know where I am. Dust and smoke cut visibility down to a few metres. Through the filter of my helmet, I smell the burning of Terra. I smell blood, too, so much blood it troubles that reality though which I move.

The walls of the Imperial Palace are a vague shape in a cloudy distance lit by the flaring streaks and blooms of fireballs. It is far from me. The fortunes of war have brought me away from what I was defending.

How can that be? And look – the Palace is too small.

I have lost my brothers. The Traitors have seized the Palace and shattered our Legion.

No. Wrong. That never happened.

I boil with the need to make betrayal pay with blood. If I am alone, I will be enough. I begin to walk. I reach a slope. I climb it. At the top, I see hulking silhouettes moving towards the walls. There is my closest enemy.

Why?

I am about to use my jump pack when I see more shapes to my right. The dust settles enough for me to see Rhinos a few dozen metres from me. More foes. Closer yet.

Why?

I take a step forward. My body locks. It holds me still. I snarl, frustrated at every second that keeps me from exacting justice. My frame quivers as the ground shakes from the artillery fire falling on all sides.

Artillery? Targeting what?

As I focus on the Rhinos, doubts catch up with my body's hesitation. Do the vehicles hold friend or foe?

Why are they not moving? Are they with the force advancing on the Palace or not?

Why are they besieging what is held?

I look towards the Palace, confused. My need to storm it is wrong. The Traitors cannot take it. I know this with a perfect certainty. What I am seeing is not possible. The situation makes no sense.

Contradictions. See the flaws. Ask the questions.

Whose is this voice? It is distant. A jagged glint in darkness. An irritant. A flaw in the Rage.

Distant but familiar. The contradictions are important. The voice wants me to see.

I have no time for it. Fury bursts through my skull. Such rage will destroy any enemy. I will burn my foe with anger alone.

Which foe?

The Rhinos? The army? The foe at the gates?

Rage needs direction.

The voice will not be silent. It lies at the bottom of a dark sea, yet it reaches past the surface. It grasps me. Why is the weak thing so strong?

Look. Look and see. Really see.

Whose voice is this? Whose voice?

Who are you?

The question is urgent. The voice is distant, but the question is too powerful to ignore. It *will* be answered.

I recognise the voice. His name is Lemartes.

I am Lemartes.

I look towards the Imperial Palace. It is shrunken

to the size of a mere mountain. As the dust clears before my eyes and in my mind, I see the pillar of blood. The source of the smell that reaches through my senses, seeking to trigger the frenzy whose suppression shapes the nobility of the Blood Angels. I understand that it is not artillery that is pounding the ground. The coherence of Terra shatters. Confusion returns.

The confusion is a form of clarity. I welcome it. The contradictions smash into each other, the waves of clashing seas. I accept the confusion, and so reject the false answers.

The depths of the Black Rage release me. I rise to light. To the real.

Who am I?

I am Chaplain Lemartes of the Blood Angels. I am the Guardian of the Lost. I am one of the Lost. My special curse is to know that I am. My blessing is to be able to act. To visit my rage and the rage of my brothers on the enemies of the Emperor.

And I have been diverted from my task.

My need to serve the Chapter brings clarity to my vision as well as my mind. As the dust settles, I see Phlegethon once more. I recognise Hive Profundis.

I see many bodies, too. Burned and smashed. They wear the uniform of the Iron Guard. Most of the corpses are in the crater. The closer they get to the site of the second impact, on the far side of the bowl, the less recognisable they are. To the east, what remains of the regiment marches on, following our forces. If Reinecker is still at their head, he and his troops are going through the motions of war. There is nothing the Mordians can do any longer. I imagine the humiliated fury Reinecker must feel. But the Rage leaves me no room for sympathy.

I can move again. I make my way to the Rhinos. They have been buffeted by the blast, their hulls scorched. They are intact, though. I advance to the front of the centre one. I stand so Orias can see me. He starts the engine.

As I head towards the rear hatch. Corbulo emerges from the thinning cloud. 'My mind is clear, brother,' I tell him. As clear as it ever is.

'What do you see?' he asks. As he must.

'Phlegethon. Profundis. Fourth Company moving towards the walls. Time slipping away.'

'I am glad to hear it.'

There is something else that requires clarity. 'I did not hear you.'

'I know.' He taps his gorget. 'My vox has been damaged.'

'Then you understand.'

He nods. 'You returned without my help. That doesn't mean my method was unsound.'

'Before the explosion, my condition was worsening. Brother, only I can pull myself free of the delusions. Perhaps you can help others. But not me.'

'You would cut yourself free from all aid?' Corbulo asks.

'It is not a choice. It is my state.' My fate.

The hatch opens. The Death Company strains at the shackles. The great wave has hit my brothers hard. Their howls are more incoherent than ever. Their rage is more intense.

But I will lead them. And we will bring ruin to the foe.

CHAPTER EIGHT

Battering the Gates

We charge through the night of fire. I ride in the open roof hatch of *Bloodpyre*. No shackles for this journey. I will see the battlefield. My wrath will travel before me.

The Rhinos advance in a staggered line. Orias has the lead. He gives us the speed we need. He drives the vehicle as if it were a Stormraven. The pitted, battered surface of the plain is nothing more than turbulence. Meteorites fall on all sides. A small one strikes the earth a dozen metres ahead. Orias takes us through the crater without slowing. As *Bloodpyre* crests the far lip, we are airborne for a moment.

I do not feel the wind of our passage. I know it is there. The night is a blurred rush. I feel the constant vibrations and sudden shocks as we crush rock and bodies beneath our treads. I stare towards the gates.

The Rhino is an extension of my will, and my will is rage. Nothing will stop us. The falling moons cannot hit us. We are too fast. Too strong. Because we are fury.

We catch up with the rest of Fourth Company. Castigon has lost a Land Raider on the journey thus far. I have seen the crushed remains of crimson power armour too. The casualties are mounting, killed by the sky.

We storm past the front ranks. Castigon has the heavy armour in position, ready for the big push. But the advance has stopped. Fourth Company cannot go any closer to the pillar of blood before their manoeuvring and combat are fatally compromised by the need to fight the Thirst. The company must wait. The Blood Disciples are still out of range of the cannons. The destruction of the last of the Mordians' long-range guns is a major loss. There would have been a role for Reinecker now. He could have had his page of glory in the war for Phlegethon.

Corbulo has been riding in the hatch of the next Rhino back. He leaps from the roof now. He will join Castigon. He will be needed here. And not even he can risk approaching the pillar as we are going to.

I look back. The Iron Guard column is still marching. I do not think it will stop with the Blood Angels. Reinecker will keep going until he finds oblivion. I wonder if there is heroism in wilful futility.

The Prophet of Blood's sermon rages on over the tempest of stone. Screeds, promises, threats, edicts, invocations, prayers: his speech is all these things. But it is not always words. He wails. He roars. He gibbers daemonic syllables. The patterns and the rhythms of his voice convey meaning. And then, with no transition, his Gothic is perfectly clear. Such a moment comes now.

'*To me!*'

The people obey.

The plain still teems with the maddened populace. No matter how many have died in the meteorite bombardment, millions remain to fuel the frenzy. The flows of the crowd are disrupted by the impacts, but now, called by the Prophet, their behaviour becomes uniform. The wrathful no longer attack. They run, all in the same direction. They stream towards the walls of Phlegethon. *Bloodpyre* surges forward in a human river. The numbers ahead of us are uncountable. Hundreds of thousands will reach the Blood Disciples before we do.

They are running to their Prophet's defence. Only the ones closest to us break from the current to hurl their bodies at the Rhinos. The vehicles crush them. The people disappear beneath the treads. Yet their acts are not sacrifices. Their rage is such that they throw themselves at the Rhinos as if they really could smash armour with mere flesh.

We are less than a thousand metres away. Orias and the other drivers risk much taking us this far. We are slamming through and over a greater and greater concentration of the wrathful. Our speed is such that we move past them as they attack us, and run down more and more of those rushing ahead of us to answer the summons. I cannot imagine what defence these weak vessels can offer the Prophet. My hand tenses around the Blood Crozius. My vision flashes with the red-black anticipation of enacted rage.

Justice for the Angel. Justice upon the Traitors.

Through all time. From any era. I will strike with anger fresh from the blow of ultimate betrayal. And with the anger matured over ten thousand years.

There is an incandescent flash to my right. At impact, my auto-senses shut out the sound and the light. I feel this wind. The pressure wave almost pulls me from the hatch. *Bloodpyre* slews hard to the right, then stops. Vision restored, I climb out and jump to the ground. There is a crater just past the Rhino's flank. The meteorite was a small one, barely enough to reach the ground without burning up. Large enough. It glanced against the side of the *Bloodpyre*. The armour is burned and dented, but the hull is intact. The treads are not.

Orias joins me. 'This is as far as I can take you, Chaplain,' he says.

'Further than I could ask,' I tell him. Further than he should have gone. His voice has a familiar tension: the conscious, desperate grip on control. He is too close to the pillar. The fragility of reason erodes him.

This close, the blood defines the world. The roar of the whirling pillar is the voice of a hurricane. The force of its blast skyward is volcanic. Volcano, storm, miracle and symbol: the blood is all these things. It is the arterial fountain of a fatally wounded world. It is also a threat and a challenge aimed at the heart of the Blood Angels.

The other two Rhinos have stopped. I vox the drivers. 'The Death Company thanks you. Return to our brothers. We will reunite for victory.'

On both sides, the mob streams past. The vehicles are stones in a foaming river.

We open the rear hatches of the Rhinos. I call to my brothers. I promise them retribution. I speak in terms those who can still understand language will receive without translation. They will hear my words, not distortions imposed by madness. As for those who do not understand, they too hear me. They hear the Black Rage speak through me. That is all they need.

I see the parallels with the Prophet of Blood. I cannot let them trouble me. We command through rage. At a level more primal than language. More powerful. I accept the similarity. It offends me. I direct that fury. This is the way of the Ruinous Powers. Of course there is resemblance. That is the great crime of the Traitors. They were once our brothers. They are degraded, fallen, deserving of nothing but extermination. The similarities between us only exacerbate the monstrosity of the offence.

My anger grows stronger even as I gather the Death Company around me. There is no blurring. I know exactly where and when I am. Good. Good.

Sanguinius, preserve my clarity of wrath.

As the Rhinos pull away, the land falls silent. The meteorite storm ends. No more drumming anthem of impacts. No more streaks in the sky.

I doubt that the last of the moons has fallen. There must still be a cloud of them encircling Phlegethon. Perhaps the usefulness of the impacts has come to an end. Perhaps the power that drew the moons down, as awesome as it must be to hurl celestial bodies at will, must concentrate itself elsewhere. I do not know the reason for the calm. I do not know the consequences for the battlefield.

None of this matters.

What matters is what the Traitors do not know.

They do not know what I can do.

The Death Company launches. We rise on arcs of fire. A new meteor storm.

'They aren't advancing,' Lhessek said. 'Why are they digging in?'

The details of movement over the blasted plain were hard to make out through the clusters of impacts and fireballs. Khevrak could see the substantial displacement of the Blood Angels, though. He could see where they had stopped. 'They can't come any closer,' he told Lhessek.

'And we wait?' Impatient again. Miracles were no longer enough for him.

'We wait.' Khevrak was hungry for war too. It would come. A very short time, and it would come.

'The Prophet's work nears completion,' Dhassaran said. 'You know this in your blood, brother.'

Lhessek grunted. 'Chance could finish them for us. One large impact.'

'There is no chance.' Dhassaran raised his arms. 'Profundis crumbles. The enemy is battered. And not a single meteorite falls close enough to do our position any damage. Is that chance? There are moons in orbit large enough to sink this continent. They do not fall. Is this chance?'

'No,' Lhessek admitted. He gestured at the hundreds of thousands of mortals gathering before the base. A hundred metres separated them from the Prophet's hill of rubble. 'Why has he called them?'

'For war,' Dhassaran said. 'For blood. For sacrifice.'

'For defence,' Khevrak said. He saw the parallel streaks of jump packs cutting the night less than a kilometre away. Almost thirty fire trails. Claws of light arcing towards the Blood Disciples' position. The gathering of the people and the end of the meteor storm fell into place. Energy was being redirected against a specific threat. 'You want vengeance?' he said to Lhessek, and pointed. 'Look. Here is your chance.' He switched to the company vox. 'Disciples of the Blood God,' he said. 'Our foes come to kill the Prophet. Give them the full measure of our wrath. Protect the Prophet at any cost!'

We descend. The Death Company acts with a perfect unity of purpose. It is more than my guidance that grants the squads this focus. It is the target himself. The Prophet calls the people of Phlegethon to him. He calls us too. His words and hymns are abominations. They share the same root as the Heresy. They share its tenets. We hear the obscenities that were shouted during the siege of the Imperial Palace. The Angel heard them aboard Horus' flagship. The speaker of lies must die. Our rage arrows us at him. It shields us from the Thirst. Ten thousand years of anger, consuming our souls, will not be diverted by degraded appetite. The pillar of blood spins and roars. Its proximity is irrelevant in this moment.

The thing that capers below us is no man. It is flesh in the grip of rage. It must be purged from existence.

My muscles tense, already experiencing the blows that will kill the Prophet. I feel the sharp crack of his skull. The resistance of his muscle. The splash of his blood. Anger races ahead of the speed of my drop. Fury alone will kill this being.

The Prophet looks up. I am still too far to see more than a monstrous suggestion of a face. But I can feel his smile. It strikes with physical force. It is almost enough to knock me off course. The Prophet extends his broken-jointed arm to my right, in the direction of the pillar of blood. He hooks it back in, as if gathering wheat, then sweeps upward. The pillar obeys his command. It sends out a limb of blood. The volume is immense. It is a river of vitae. A lake. It falls upon the thronging mob. It gathers them.

We confront yet another of the day's black wonders.

An immense wave of blood and bodies rises to meet us. It reflects the glow of the night's guttering fires. It is black, tinted red. The wave is a wall, a barrier and a trap. Its mass blocks our approach to the Prophet, and it comes to devour us. Thousands upon thousands of the wrathful reach out to grasp us.

I slam into the wave. Struggling, broken, drowning bodies clutch. I sink into crimson-flecked darkness and the coiling, tangling nest of limbs.

The blur.

Another plunge. Another ocean.

Blur of soul and mind and world and time and...

No.

This mire is dangerous in ways much more than physical. I have been swallowed by the material incarnation of the entangling, sucking ocean of the Black Rage. If I do not emerge soon, I will cease to know the difference between my mind and the world. I thrash. I rip arms from their sockets and break bones. I fire up the jump pack. It incinerates the bodies beneath it. I move, though I am unsure of the direction. I am unstinting with the promethium. The temperature rises. Flesh burns. Blood boils. And then I am free.

I rise above the wave. Some of my brothers, but not all, have pulled themselves out too. I push the jump higher. I will pass over the wave.

It rises higher still. It cannot be avoided. It comes for me a second time.

Very well. Then I will go through.

'Tear the enemy lies to shreds,' I call to my brothers. 'Confront them and shatter their strength.'

I change the direction of my flight. I hit the wave at full speed, Blood Crozius extended. I leave my bolt pistol maglocked to my thigh, keeping my left hand free to crush and tear. I leave a crater of flesh in my wake. I slow down as I go deeper and deeper into the convulsing, seething mass. The people care more to hold me than they do to breathe. They are mindless rage.

Forward. Killing. Focused wrath against the unreasoning. The Blood Crozius is the only light in this crushing night. The wave and its hands would drown me twice over. I am too strong for it. Twice over. My strength of arms rips bodies apart, and my strength of rage turns away all attempts to submerge it in a larger, undifferentiated anger. The Crozius severs and crushes. It is powerful in its anger. Its sacredness is blinding. There is no leverage in this shifting mass of vitae and limbs. The relic I wield needs none. I am deep within the daemonic, and everything the Crozius touches is a target. Tainted blood boils on contact. Corrupted mortals come apart.

Forward. Always forward. The wave heaves up and down, an animal in convulsions. I do not know what direction I am facing. But it is forward. The grasping wave cannot make me retreat. I am on the offensive. I am the cancer inside its body. It sought to consume me. But I am its punishment.

Forward. Though I move through liquid, I hear the

splintering and cracking of bones. There are circular motions around me now. A current in the blood breaking the bodies, pressing them around me. A tightening spiral. Constrictor. The pressure around my limbs is so great I can feel it through my armour. It slows me down. I shred the coils. Keep moving, tugged at by thick viscosity. The stench of corrupted blood is a fist inside my skull. There is no summons to frenzy. There is only a damp, suffocating foulness. It is one with the darkness clamping down on me.

In these depths, I can still hear the voice of the Prophet. His sermon continues without cease. I counter with my own prayers. I vox them to the squads. Let those who hear me draw strength. 'My arm is for the Emperor. My arm is for Sanguinius. My rage is for them both. For betrayed father and murdered brother. My rage is my strength. Time does not fade the crime of betrayal. Let my every action be the violence of retribution. Brothers, strike with me. We are in the grip of the daemonic. Teach it the meaning of vengeance.'

The coils tighten. They fuel my outrage. The Blood Crozius is bright as burning plasma. The crimson behind my eyes flashes brighter. Anger takes more and more and more of consciousness. The undertow of madness clutches me. I break its hold as I break through the bodies. There is nothing here for the delusion to build on. No sight to transform into the sites of our great tragedies. My sermon becomes an unending snarl.

It too is a prayer.

Then I am through. I part bodies like a curtain, and I plunge down the other side of the wave. To my left, my right, above and below, the Death Company punches through the barrier. We drop amidst a wonder of our own making: blood is bleeding. A cataract of blood pours from the wave. The barrier loses its coherence. It has failed in its purpose.

I land on my feet. The earth shakes as the wave collapses, slamming a hundred thousand bodies to the ground. A surge of blood washes past my boots and laps at the foot of the Prophet's rubble.

Our target is less than fifty metres away.

The final moments of the moon storm took even more of a toll on the 237th Regiment. Reinecker supposed they were fortunate, though the word no longer had any meaning that he understood. There had been no direct hits. A few near misses whose blasts had still been enough to kill the soldiers closest to them. He had refused to stop and seek shelter with the Blood Angels.

'Why would we?' he'd said to Stromberg. 'They're as likely to kill us as what's falling from the sky.'

He'd led the column on, and the storm had ended. The way forward was the clearest he'd seen it. The wrathful were ignoring the Mordians. They were all running forward in answer to the summons of the monster preacher.

This was the closest Reinecker had come to the

pillar of blood. He felt its terrible pull. He felt what little temper he had left fray with every step he took in its direction. The discipline of his training gave him the reserves he needed to stay calm. Barely. He tried not to look at the pillar. It was so huge now, though, that it was always there at the edge of his vision.

Reinecker looked back. The Blood Angels were not advancing. 'What are they waiting for?' he said.

Stromberg said, 'Do they expect the enemy to come to them?'

'Why would that happen?'

No answer to that. He didn't expect there to be. Then the nightmarish company of the Blood Angels, the madmen in black armour, passed overhead. He watched their flight towards the Traitors. And then...

Then...

A wave. A wall of bodies and blood. He stood rooted to the spot. Stromberg was silent beside him. They stared. Silent, horrified awe swept the regiment. Reinecker watched, and felt something die inside. He held the implications of the monstrous impossibility at bay. He was no ecclesiarch. It did not fall to him to explain. That was the duty of someone else. 'Get me Auberlen,' he said.

Stromberg blinked, tore her eyes away from the horror, and walked back down the length of the column. She returned a few minutes later with the preacher. His face was pinched. He was no longer turning away from the pillar. His gaze was riveted by it. He made Reinecker think of an animal confronted by its predator.

'Do you still maintain that is an illusion?' Reinecker asked. 'The Blood Angels just flew into it.'

Auberlen didn't look at him. 'No,' he said in a cracked whisper. 'It is not an illusion.'

'Then what is it?'

For a long moment, Auberlen said nothing. When he moved his lips, no sound emerged.

Reinecker grabbed his robes and pulled him forward. '*What is it?*'

Auberlen moved his lips again. This time, a word crept out. 'Daemonic.'

Reinecker released him. He took a step back. He turned to Stromberg. Her face was as grey as his own must have been. But she did not look surprised to have official Imperial doctrine contradicted, and a myth confirmed. 'You know of such things?'

She nodded. 'At the schola progenium,' she began, then trailed off. 'I never thought I'd see...'

All lies, then. Fundamental tenets he had believed in and fought for his entire life. He had known there could be no theologically acceptable explanation for what was happening on Phlegethon. But he had managed to hold off the full implications of that knowledge. He had worked hard to compartmentalise the terrible sights. Let the Ecclesiarchy explain them when it chose to. As long as he told himself that the Adeptus Ministorum *could* account for the manifestation, he had been able to keep something like hope alive. Now it was all gone.

The great blood wave collapsed. The crunch of

shattered bodies travelled over the plain. It was followed by the sound of gunfire. The Blood Angels had engaged the Traitors. Reinecker watched.

'Colonel?' Stromberg prompted him to lead.

Reinecker thought about shooting Auberlen. He held back, barely. Anger coiled in his chest. It was iron. It had fangs. It used defeat, despair and terror as its building blocks, though it had its own identity. It would have been present had the campaign been triumphant. But now, all his defences against blind rage were tumbling. Only discipline remained.

He shoved Auberlen away. 'You have failed us,' he said. 'What good are you? Our need is greatest, and what do you offer?'

Auberlen said nothing. He kept staring at the pillar.

'Colonel,' Stromberg said again. Her voice was sharp now. She had put away her bolt pistol when the wrathful had abandoned all attacks against the regiment. Her hand hovered over the holster.

Reinecker wondered if she was that close to ending his command. Her eyes were narrowed, her lips pursed with strain. He realised that she was concentrating on holding back her own rage. They were all being worn down by this cursed world.

As he watched Stromberg struggle, he remembered his own restraint earlier. He remembered the sense of justified pride and victory that had followed. The glow of revelation yet to be comprehended.

With his back to the pillar of blood, but its roar always present, inescapable, he understood. The act of turning from rage on Phlegethon was a heroic triumph. And who was left on the planet still capable of doing so? Who could resist the triumph of wrath?

We can, he thought. *We must.*

Only discipline remained? That was enough. That was more than enough. That was the great weapon of the Mordian Iron Guard. And though the regiment was diminished, it was still the 237th. It still flew its banners. It was still the Iron Guard. And its warriors still numbered in the thousands.

He looked at the flashes and explosions of the Blood Angels' battle with the Traitors. The monsters were fighting the monsters again. If he marched the Iron Guard into a conflict between those two forces for a second time, he was asking for his troops to be slaughtered. But the mob was advancing into the fray too. That was where the battle was, and that was where the duty of the Iron Guard lay. He saw too, at last, how misplaced his pride had been before. It had been directed towards the personal glory of the grand victory. True, honest pride lay in embodying the truths of the regiment.

And so he turned to look at his troops. The emotional gravitation of the pillar was immense, but he rejected it. He clutched the discipline that was his birthright, and he gazed with saving pride on the regiment. 'Warriors of the 237th,' he shouted. 'Reject this terror! We are cold and we are discipline, and we are order. Will you march with me for Mordian and the Emperor?'

'*We march with you!*' they shouted.

'To what end?' Stromberg asked, her voice low so only he could hear.

To what practical end, he didn't know. He had faith, though, that the Emperor's design for the regiment would be revealed as the last force of sanity entered the heart of the fray. But there was one goal that was clear now. Reinecker said, 'We march to redemption.'

Stromberg smiled.

The Blood Disciples are ready. They come at us in force. We are scattered from our passage though the barrier. They outnumber us, and move to overwhelm before we can regroup.

They had time to manoeuvre their vehicles while we were caught in the wave. They moved the Predators apart. Now the tanks come in from the left and right while the Disciples keep us engaged. The Rhinos guard the approach to the Prophet's hill.

I am near the left-hand end of our ragged column. Two Blood Disciples rush me with bolter fire. The Predator closes in. It crushes Quirinus before he can retaliate. Its treads run over the former Reclusiarch's torso. He still moves after its passage. There is nothing left of him from the chest down, only smashed ceramite and bone, but he raises an arm to fire at the Traitors who come at him. They finish him off. But still he fired. The final act of a brother who believed Mephiston to be more monstrous than the Rage itself.

Bolter shells strike my chest plate. One punches through a weakened portion. I am injured. A flare of pain. A greater burst of rage. I throw myself to the right, out of their stream of fire. I rise and charge them. They alter their angle of approach. The momentum is now mine. We close too fast for them to take me down with gunfire. I fall on them with a howl of thunder. I sweep the Blood Crozius in. It is so charged by my rage that its light could trigger photolens defences. I think it does. My target stumbles before its glory. I strike the side of his helmet. A single blow. It takes the top half of his skull off.

Still charging. The body of my first kill has yet to fall. I hit the other like a battering ram. I carry him backwards into the path of the Predator. Its autocannon fires. A long-range weapon attempting the point-blank kill. The gunner willing to sacrifice his brother to get to me. Too late. The explosion is behind me. I smash the Traitor against the hull of the Predator. Metre-long spikes cover its surface. The ragged, leathered skins of the Blood Disciples' victims hang from the spikes. They are trophies, banners of atrocity. The lower hull, beneath the autocannon, leads with a jagged-toothed edge.

I break him backwards over the tank. I dig my feet into the ground. The tank pushes me backwards. With difficulty. The impact of the collision ruptures the Traitor's jump pack. Fire engulfs us both. A spike has impaled him through the seams of his armour beneath the right shoulder. He cannot get an angle of fire with his bolter and tries to batter me away with it. I hit him with the Blood Crozius. Again and again. The streak of its anger is so fast, so bright, that I can barely see the damage I am doing. I sever one arm. Then the other. Then I smash his chest until the armour cracks like an egg and I turn his hearts into smoke and ash.

The Predator comes to a halt.

I climb over the Traitor's body onto the hull of the Predator. I grasp the autocannon and pull myself onto the turret. Halfway out the hatch, a Traitor is waiting for me. He swings his chainaxe. It hits my shoulder. The impact is hard and grinding. I drop, falling faster than the blade before it can cut through my armour. The turret swings hard. I slide off. I fall back to the front hull. The Blood Disciple follows. The spikes arrest my fall. The Traitor raises the chainaxe over his head. Its arc will shatter my skull. I grab a spike and lunge forward, striking at his legs with the Crozius. I hit him hard enough to spoil his blow. He stumbles and grabs the autocannon for support. I rise faster.

My first strike breaks open his helmet. My second finishes him.

I make my way back to the turret. I pause at the hatch. I survey the battlefield. The Blood Disciples and the Death Company clash on the ground and in the air. I have lost three brothers. Their runes have turned red in my auto-senses. There are more bodies of Blood Disciples. We are holding our own. But we are not advancing. The Traitors are holding us back from the Prophet.

I tear open the hatch. The Predator is still motionless. So is the turret now, but since it moved during the struggle, I must have been attacked by the driver, rather than the gunner. I am about to drop into the tank. Then I change my mind. I toss in a frag grenade instead. Just before it goes off, I fire my jump pack. My flight is a short one. I land back on the hull just as the grenade goes off.

I have made what will appear to be a mistake. The grenade will damage the interior, but it is an anti-personnel device, not a siege weapon. It is also not likely to kill a Space Marine. I want him to see the mistake. I want him to think me gone. I want him to leave the turret and start the engine again.

He does.

With a jolt, the Predator moves forward into the fray once more. It slews back and forth a bit, confirming my surmise. The gunner is now driving. Ahead, the other tank is fighting several of my brothers. Its autocannon fires. Its shell strikes a Blood Disciple and a Blood Angel in midair. They fall to the ground, still grappling. The next few moments will see one or both killed.

I cannot take the time to concern myself with either possibility. Right now, this vehicle is our best chance at killing the Prophet.

Now I go inside. The compartment is crowded and damaged. Control surfaces for the turret are

scorched. I make my way to the driver's compartment, a tiny blister in the lower front of the tank. The
Blood Disciple turns at my approach. He grabs his
bolt pistol. I already have mine in hand. There is no
room to swing the Crozius in here. I pour shells into
the gunner. I kill him before he can rise. He slumps
over the controls, his weight pushing on the stick.

The Predator surges forward.

I lean into the blister, push the corpse to one side
and look out the viewing block. The vehicle is still on
a course to meet up with the other. It disgusts me to
touch anything contaminated by the daemonic. The
interior of the tank is draped with more tanned hides,
more empty faces screaming their endless final grief.
The machine-spirit of the Predator is a corruption.
I can sense its fury at my presence. Nevertheless, I
reach past the body and grasp the steering. I make a
correction. The movement is crude, but it is enough. I
will not soil my gauntlets further. But I am forcing the
Predator to betray its masters. That is very like justice.

The weight of the dead gunner on the controls is
enough to ensure forward movement. I climb back
onto the roof. The tank is now angled towards our
target. It roars towards the Rhinos. I crouch on the
turret, motionless, waiting my chance. I need just a
few more seconds. This struggle has been reduced
to that small moment of time. If we gain that much
of an advantage over the Blood Disciples, it is all we
will need to kill the Prophet. The margin is a thin
one. The Traitors cannot afford any mistake. Now I

have seized one of their vehicles. So they have seconds to realise and stop my advance.

The seconds pass.

On my right, to the west, the mob closes in again. The wrathful must cross a marshy wasteland made of the pulped bodies of their fellow citizens. They run, answering the call of the Prophet. They, also, are too late. The seconds are done.

The Blood Disciples realise what I am doing. The Rhinos open fire. The other Predator swings its autocannon around. But I am through the lines. The bulk of the fighting is behind me. I jump from the turret as the Rhino combi-bolter shells shriek above it. The autocannon blasts the turret directly, destroying it. But I am in the air, rising. The Prophet will fall.

Another figure shoots up to intercept me. He was behind the Rhinos, hanging back to protect the Prophet. We collide, grapple, and plunge back to earth. I try to direct our fall at the Prophet himself. My opponent deflects our flight enough that we strike the mound halfway down from the top. Rockcrete powders from the force of our landing. We stand and face each other. In his right hand, he holds a defiled crozius. This creature of the burning eyes and mutilated features was once a Chaplain. He has done worse than abandon his duties. He has perverted them. There can hardly be a more debased form of Traitor. My rage finds new peaks of intensity. Language cannot encompass the contempt and hatred I have for this being, and I raise the Blood Crozius in silence. He meets my blow with his foul symbol. The clash unleashes a flash of light that explodes over the entire battlefield.

Red light and black.

Searing blood and shining void.

Faith against faith, wrath against wrath.

In that flash, the battlefield is frozen. Every detail of war etched in stark crimson and night. I am aware of a simultaneity of events. Of an accumulation.

Of completion.

The Death Company and the Blood Disciples wage battle with the full might of their faith and the perfection of rage.

The mob is in the midst of all. The humans are killed by every act of either my brothers or the Traitors. They burn in the backwash of jump packs. They are crushed beneath ceramite boots when the combatants descend. Their flesh is pulverised in crossfires. The sweeping blows in close-quarters combat cut them down. They are insects, in the way, barely noticed. But they bleed. They die for a reason. Something notices.

And the mortals are dying in huge numbers. They are being killed by a force coming up from behind them.

The Iron Guard. They add to the blood being spilled.

So we have all played our part.

Critical mass is reached. Now the final act begins.

The darkness lightens. Perhaps dawn is breaking beyond the cloud cover, but the light that falls on us is crimson. The entire sky stains red as the pillar of blood rushes up, leaving the ground entirely. A deep wound in the earth remains in its wake. The vitae spreads across the firmament. The clouds are heavy with blood in an instant. There is a fraction of a second of suspension. The world waits beneath a crimson dome. The time is long enough only for me to bring the Blood Crozius back for another strike at the Blood Disciple. It feels like an age. There is so much weight. I will fight this Traitor. I will give my life to kill the Prophet. But I know I am too late.

The moment ends. The skies open. The deluge is here.

The blood fell everywhere. Over the plains of Profundis. Over the burning ruins of Corymbus. Over every land mass of Phlegethon. Over the oceans too, and where the blood touched water, the water became blood. Billions had died when the moons had plunged to the surface. Billions had survived, the alchemy of tragedy taking despair, grief and terror and turning them into rage. And now the billions drowned. Flash floods roared through ruined streets. The underhives filled rapidly, subterranean oceans rising in darkness. Craters became lakes. Plains became seas.

At Hive Dacrima, the people stopped tearing at each other. They saw the new inland sea turn crimson. They were slicked by the downpour. They slid in the cascades that washed down from roofs. They watched in terror as the sea rose, lapping first at the city's ruined walls, then reaching further and further into the streets. They did not think to look up into the mountains. They did not think about the streams and rivers that burst their banks within the first few minutes of the bloodfall.

The rioters in the upper reaches of the city had a warning. They heard a rushing rumble over the constant drumming and sheeting of the falling blood. Some looked. They saw a huge, boiling wave come surging through the mountain pass. It was twenty metres high. Funnelled by steep valleys, it raced to the city with the speed of a maglev train. The people who saw it were the ones who had time to scream, to give full expression to their horror and rage. Then they were swept away by the great flood. The streets were narrow. They forced the surge higher. The pressure of the impact collapsed rockcrete. The towers of Dacrima fell. The city vanished beneath red waves.

Rage had draped the planet. Rage had spilled blood, so much blood that it covered the globe. Phlegethon became the perfect sacrifice to the Blood God.

Everything that came before was prologue. Even the meteor storm is reduced by the total, all-encompassing nature of what falls on us now. The blood is everywhere. The blood is all. The world vanishes in the torrents. At the centre of all, on the mound of the Prophet, the fall of blood is massive, concentrated, opaque. It is as if the pillar had returned, reversing its direction to strike downward from the sky. It cannot be withstood. The Blood Disciple and I are battered down and carried off. I am submerged again. The blood smashes me against rubble. It hurls me back from the walls. I am caught by blood, pulled by blood. But I will not be drowned by blood.

My doom is other. It is rage.

The flood releases me as it spreads out over the plain. I stand. The blood here is ankle deep. I look through sheets pouring from the sky as through thick veils and fog. The contours of reality are soft, uncertain. The figures moving in the crimson limbo are silhouettes of war. Red and black. All I see is red and black.

I know this vision. I know this world. It is the madness from behind my eyes brought into the real. I must deny it. I defy the distortion.

No.

No.

No.

But this time denial is madness, because the madness is true. This is the world in which I must fight. Perhaps I alone can do so and win, because I have been before, and will return again. The day will come when I shall never leave it. But not this day, I vow. I will not let my brothers come to their end here.

And worse will follow. If this vision has taken form, there is another, more terrible yet, that is coming. The blood rises. It will become a lake, and then a sea. The sight that assailed me on Baal will find me here. It will find us all.

The bloodfall has pushed the Death Company back, robbing us of the ground we had gained. It knocked my brothers out of the sky, and the wave carried them out to where I now stand. We push ourselves forward through the torrent from above. The land has become a crimson marsh. My boots sink with a sucking sound. I walk upon the festering, rotting flesh of the world. After the first smash, the downpour lessens slightly. Or perhaps I adjust to the new, blood-soaked world. I can see more clearly. The silhouettes acquire detail. I can make out the Blood Disciples. They are still clustered near their Prophet. The blood did not sweep them away. That the force of the rain could be directed to affect us, and us alone, tells me more about the huge strength of the power we are fighting. That the worst of the bloodfall was its arrival tells me something else. If we have not drowned in vitae yet, there are limits to this evil strength.

Many of the mortals, however, have drowned. Their corpses float face-down in the mire. Most can barely stand under the onslaught of vitae. They stumble and crawl forward. They choke on the blood. Some vomit it up. Others collapse beneath the weight of the deluge and die, their hands still clasped as they offer the worship of rage to the Prophet.

Reinecker and the Iron Guard are transfixed. The regiment is not far from me. Their silhouettes are motionless. Their postures are angular with tension.

They are agonised statues of bronze. Though they remain upright, they are paralysed.

I believe I know why.

They are immobilised by the paroxysm of rage that has taken them. Their bodies can barely contain the fury. It is beyond expression in its first true flowering. It is a lightning strike.

The Mordians have a taste of the burden of the Blood Angels. They are mortals. They are helpless before its assault.

Or so I think.

But then, incredibly, the column begins to move. The Iron Guard advances. Not as a wrathful mob. As a coherent military unit. Though I wonder how long they can continue in this way, I am amazed.

I wonder: do I see cause for hope?

If I do, it is a thin one, overwhelmed by what I hear next. The company vox-channel explodes with shouts and snarls. Voices call for faith. For discipline. There is a pleading to brothers. Not for mercy, but for reason. The voices dissolve into more snarls. One continues to ring clear: Corbulo's. I hear enough. I know that the Red Thirst is rampant in Fourth Company.

The rain falls. The blood rises. The Blood Disciples gather around the hill of rubble. The misshapen Prophet no longer dances. He is still, his work done. The peak of the rubble collapses, plunging into the interior of the hill. The Prophet vanishes into the broken rockcrete. The stacked wreckage now resembles a volcano. Or a burial mound.

I know that hill is both.

'*Hold, brothers!*' I vox to the Death Company. We must not attack without knowing the full extent of the threat. '*Let the enemy reveal himself.*' The words I speak are more prayers than commands. I cannot expect them to be understood. At the level of our shared madness, though, they are. My will directs the focus of the cursed. They respond to my words, as the mob responded to the Prophet. The damned of the Death Company move to my position. I am their guarantor of vengeance.

The blood pours into the mound. Enough to drown the mortal. Enough to finish that creature's journey at long last. The mound shakes. Eldritch lightning crackles around its width, and lashes the Blood Disciples. The Prophet's sermon has ceased. In the vacuum created by its sudden silence comes a different voice. It is louder, deeper. It is the sound of tectonic plates grinding against each other. It emerges from the mound, but it reverberates through the air, the rain of blood, the ground itself. No sermon from this voice, no exhortation, no call. No words at all. Only a growl building to a roar. It is grief, loss, rage. The emotions are disturbing in their familiarity. I must refuse the bond they seek to forge. I find the difference: the growl is also mindless.

The mound shakes. The movement ripples outward. The tremors reach me. They race past. They bring the touch of dark power across the plain. The mound shakes again, violently. A death throe.

The hill of rubble bursts apart. Chunks of rockcrete fly in all directions. There is a flash of energy that is not light, yet it blinds. It is red and it is black, and it is both, and it is no colour at all. My photolenses do not recognise it, and I am dazzled. I keep staring. I will have clarity. I will see this to the end.

And when the false light fades, the enemy is revealed. He stands upon the ruin of the mound. He towers over the Blood Disciples. He is the mindless perfection of rage.

Skarbrand.

CHAPTER NINE

Redemption

The colossus of rage roared, and the planet shook. Skarbrand spread his wings. Their span was huge, majestic. Yet they were torn, ragged. The blood rain fell through the rents in their dark flesh. They were banners of tragedy. His hide was the red of exposed muscle. He was a monster of blood, nourished by blood, standing in the endless deluge of blood. In each hand, he carried an axe. Their blades were almost as large as Khevrak.

The captain of the Blood Disciples watched as Skarbrand raised the axes high and brought them down, hacking deep into the earth. Still he roared. He roared with the thunder of absolute wrath, with the shattering of grief and loss, and with the hurricane chaos of a mind that was gone forever.

Skarbrand roared, and the moment of transcendence had come. Khevrak felt the hand of his god reach into his core. The warp broke through the real and began his metamorphosis. His bones flowed with change. They grew longer. They thickened. They twisted. They sprouted new growths. Agony speared his frame. His mouth jerked open in shock. His helmet was suddenly too small. His skull was expanding, pushing against the interior. He grunted and struggled to remove the helmet. It was already too late. The pressure built. He heard cracks. He felt movement where none should be. He took a staggering step forward. He clutched his helmet as if he might contain the lethal expansion.

'*Redemption!*' Dhassaran shrieked in pain and triumph. '*Redemption!*'

Khevrak tried to echo him. But his tongue was tangled in his lengthening fangs. Lances of glowing pain shot through his vision. The cracking grew louder, filling his ears.

'*Redemption!*' The cry cut through the pain. And the roar of Skarbrand rumbled over all.

Khevrak formed the word. 'Redemption.' The syllables were hard, jagged as shattered bone. They tumbled away from him. So did meaning. He took another step. It felt like his last. His body pushed against his armour in all directions. Bones turned back on themselves, slicing through muscle and nerves. 'Redemption.' Just noises now. No meaning at all. Dhassaran was wrong.

There was meaning in what he heard. The meaning was in Skarbrand's roar. The loss. The grief. There was no redemption there. There was atonement without end for a crime that could never be expiated. There was meaning in the daemon that had manifested among the Blood Disciples.

Khevrak fell to his knees. The pressure in his head felt as if a power claw were squeezing his skull. The cracking multiplied. Bone and ceramite broke and fused. Shards stabbed him behind the eyes, through the temple, backwards into his jaw.

If this was transcendence, it was transcendent punishment. He was being transfigured into the shape of penalty.

Why was there grief in the great daemon lord's wrath? Why was there loss? Because he had sinned against the Blood God. Manipulated by Tzeentch, goaded into a rage beyond control or sense, he had dared raise his hand against Khorne. One blow. One single, irrevocable moment of berserk folly. Khorne had hurled him across the warp, into exile, into an inferno of wrath, self-loathing, and eternally futile atonement. He bore the mark of his chastisement on his wings and in his broken mind. There could be no forgiveness from Khorne. Not from the being who was rage itself. There was no redemption. There was only the quest for it, the duty to struggle for what would never be granted. The struggle had no alternative. To turn from that path was apostasy, and would invite even more terrible retribution.

Even now, even consumed by an anguish that dwarfed what he had undergone in the transformation from mortal to Space Marine, Khevrak's worship did not waver. He saw the extent of his sin. The act that had made him a Blood Disciple could not be expunged. It was his original sin.

'*Redemption!*' he cried, and the word had meaning again. He understood why Dhassaran shrieked it. He was pleading to continue the quest, to feel all the pain of seeking what would always be out of reach, because to do so was to be the faithful servant of the Blood God. Let him feel despair. Let it fuel his rage. Let him shed blood as never before, consumed by the knowledge that it would never be enough.

This was the transcendence of the Blood Disciples. Their form would be shaped by the crime that created them. Like Skarbrand, they had struck a forbidden blow. That they had killed the first Prophet of Blood while still acting as agents of the Imperium was no mitigation. They had sinned against Khorne.

He spread his arms. '*Redemption!*' He embraced the truth of his transgression, of the Blood Disciples' original sin that gave him meaning. He embraced the pain. He immolated the last of hope. Despair smothered its embers. And then a new fire erupted. It was a rage greater than he had known before. The rage agonised by its own failure ever to cause enough pain. The rage whose failure would push it always and forever towards unreachable limits.

Redemption was a wail. It was the punishment he would share with Skarbrand. It was the bitterness he would spread to the universe.

As his mind was consumed by flame, Khevrak understood at the most profound level his need to burn.

His next cry was not a word. It was a battle roar hungry for the blood of the galaxy. It was also the sound of the perfect agony of birth.

His helmet blew apart. His chest plate cracked down the centre. On his arms and legs, his armour split into sections. They sank into his flesh as his limbs continued to grow. The agony continued, but it did not kill him. The transfiguration, unimpeded, accelerated. He had passed the test and earned the full privilege of his curse.

The blood poured down. Red from a red sky, the air soaked red, the ground foaming red. The red of sacrifice and anger and war and fire. The red that was promised to the materium. Blood washed over Khevrak's changing skull. He opened his mouth that was now a maw. He drank the blood. It made him thirst for more.

Around him, his fellow Disciples proved themselves worthy or lacking. There were many failures. As he contorted, he knew contempt for the warriors who did not have the strength of soul to endure their lot. Two were almost entirely contained by their armour. They expanded and twisted until they were compressed to pulp by their own growth. Bubbling flesh oozed from the seams of their armour. Their corpses gradually sank into the rising blood. Many others had survived, but their bodies were running riot. They sprouted multiple limbs, second heads, hooves growing from their mouths, antlers of gnarled flesh from their eyes. The legs of Bhellan had fused, turning into a serpent's tail five metres long. His upper torso was a confusion of tentacles and pincers. His head was a snapping, crocodilian maw with no eyes or brain.

And Grezhen. He had become a thing of muscle. His skeletal structure was gone. His limbs were sinew and flesh so tightly wound that it held shape without bone. His torso had grown to a mass the size of a Dreadnought. His limbs had the strength to raise the body off the ground, and they dragged him forward with the motion of scuttling fingers. He had no head, and yet from deep inside his bulk came moans. They were muffled, tortured sounds of a mouth that could never open, a hunger that could never sink teeth into flesh.

And Xever. He still walked on two legs. He still had arms. He still had a head. But his skull was a shifting cluster of jaws. Their number and location changed from moment to moment. A single one parted his head on a diagonal, gaping wide to swallow the blood. Then there were four, craters with razored teeth chattering at nothing. And then another change, and another, each form dying in the moment it became apparent. His neck was as long as his arm. In the centre of his throat was a single giant eye. Its two pupils merged and split like warring protozoa with each blink. Its iris was a whirling slick of yellow and red.

Disciple after Disciple mutated beyond reason or volition. They were transfigured without transcendence. Their identities were destroyed. They were rage and flesh and nothing else. They lived, though. Khevrak saw them and he judged them. His change continued, his pain savaged his mind, but he judged them. He was growing stronger. His new self was becoming concrete. *You will serve,* he thought. Soon he would speak the commands again. Already, he foresaw uses for his failed brothers.

And then there were the true Disciples. The warriors whose strength of rage and faith, like his, saw them through the test. Dhassaran, Lhessek and a few other chosen of Khorne were becoming their greater selves. There was no one form to their mutations. Their horns were variations of wrath. Khevrak's grew forward from his forehead. They extended a full metre. They were sharp as lightning claws. Eight horns surrounded Dhassaran's head. They grew into each other. They coiled, tangled. One was a spiral. Their cluster was a larger echo of his rosarius. His body was becoming the expression of his faith.

Lhessek had merged with his chainaxe. His right arm now ended in the blade. The axe head was covered in flesh. The teeth had become claws. They still whirred. There was still a motor. It made the sickening grind-crack of gears formed from bone.

Khevrak's pain abated, though it did not end. It was there to be his goad and talisman of punishment. It crawled over his spine to his skull, then down into his limbs. It was a segmented insect dragging claws through his being. His transformation ended. His flesh and armour were one. His jaws were a predator's gape. His tongue, serpent long, had a stinger. He could not speak.

And yet he did.

Dhassaran had fallen silent in the latter stages of his change. He no longer led the choir of rage. Khevrak spoke. He was captain of the Blood Disciples. He was first among the servants of the lord that had come among them. And so, he was first to speak. He led the new choir.

'*Transcendence!*' he shouted. They had come to Phlegethon seeking that state. They had found it. In all its bitterness, in all its rewards.

'*Transcendence!*' came the answer from the Blood Disciples who had joined him in the new plane of rage.

Skarbrand paid no attention to Khevrak or the others. His eyes were blank, though he stared forward with the fixity of obsession. Only a few seconds had passed since his axes had struck the ground. He raised them now, leaving deep wounds that blood rushed to fill. The furrows spread, then lengthened. They shot forward, crackling with warp fire. The earth ripped, and ripped again. The plain rippled, roiling the surface of the deepening blood slick. The unforgiven daemon lord was still the conduit of his master's will. A new miracle was set in motion.

On the plain, the people of Profundis celebrated

the arrival of the embodiment of mindless rage by turning on each other. The Mordian Iron Guard stood in their midst, completing their own spiritual journey. Further on were two factions of Blood Angels. The warriors in black had grouped together, and were advancing through the rain. Beyond them, the larger force had not moved. Khevrak sensed that disaster had come upon the enemy. Now he would bring worse.

And so to war.

The rain fell, and so did the Knights of Baal.

When the sky turned crimson, Corbulo knew what was coming. They all did. He saw the anguish on Castigon's face. The Lord Adjudicator turned to him and said, 'It falls to you to save us, Brother Corbulo.'

'The vehicles,' Corbulo began, and then the blood was there, hammering down with the force of heavy stubbers. There was no time to react.

When the blood hit his face, the Red Thirst overcame him. He was braced, and fought back. He snarled. His lips pulled apart and his neck arched as his body sought to drink the vitae falling from the clouds. He clenched his teeth, grimacing with effort to deny his instincts. He held the Red Grail. Through the haze that covered his eyes and his mind, he forced himself to feel its weight in his hand. The weight of the Blood Angels' nobility. The sum of their greatness beyond the Flaw. The weight of the duty to Sanguinius.

The weight was immense. The Grail hauled his centre of gravity forward.

With a cry, he dropped to his knees and hunched forward. The blood drummed against his head and the back of his neck. His eyes were on the Grail now. The Thirst tore at his throat. His mouth watered. His body shook with the need to rend prey and feast on its life. But his eyes were on the Grail.

'Father,' he prayed to Sanguinius, 'grant me your strength.' The words came in gasps. But they were words. He made himself say them. He was surrounded by the growls of his brothers. They had lost the power of speech. His prayer was his link to reason. 'Father,' he croaked, 'show us that we are greater than the Flaw. Give us the means to be worthy of you.'

He trembled with the effort to resist the call of the blood. He stared at the Red Grail. He narrowed his focus to that singular point of reality. He was nothing. His hunger was nothing. His body did not exist. The pain of Fourth Company did not exist. There was only the holy relic and its connection to the primarch. The Grail's deep aura of pure blood reached out to him. It enveloped him. His soul calmed. The Red Thirst receded. His mind became his own again. So did his body.

He stood, holding the Grail in front of him. Blood drenched him. It began to fill the bowl of the crater. He kept his eyes on the Grail. He saw its glow around his body, a spiritual shield against the daemonic blood. He walked with a measured pace towards the nearest Rhino. It was *Honoured End*, one of the Death Company transports. Its hatch opened as he approached. When he entered, he risked looking away from the Grail. The Thirst was there in the background, ready for a lapse of concentration. He wiped the worst of the blood from his face, and the curse withdrew further.

He made his way forward and banged on the door to the driver's compartment.

Forcas opened it. His eyes were clear, though he was ready to subdue Corbulo. He lowered his hands when he realised there was no need. 'High Priest,' he said, 'you...' He hesitated.

'I hold the Thirst at bay, brother.' He climbed inside. 'You haven't suffered any effects of this rain of blood?'

'I have resisted. So have all the other drivers.'

Corbulo wondered why that was. The blood did not work through direct contact. The pilots of the Stormravens had been affected, as had all the Blood Angels in close proximity to the pillar of blood. And most of the company now was helmeted. But the Thirst was running rampant through the Blood Angels. 'You say you resisted,' Corbulo said. 'You felt the effects, then.'

Forcas nodded. 'I still do. But I honour the primarch. I have faith in the strength he has given us. I can hold out.'

'Dilution,' Corbulo mused. The pillar had been a much more concentrated manifestation of the phenomenon. Perhaps the heavier shielding of the vehicles was enough. 'We must preserve what we can,' he said. 'Beginning with the captain.' He headed back to the rear entrance. He looked for Castigon. Visibility was minimal, but he spotted the shape of the captain's iron halo. Castigon had climbed out of the crater. There were still many civilians in the vicinity. Profundis had poured an inexhaustible supply of victims onto the plain. Castigon had joined with the rest of the Knights of Baal in their slaughter.

The cursed killing the cursed.

Corbulo pointed him out to Forcas. 'Take us there,' he said. 'I'll do the rest.'

Forcas nodded. He returned to his compartment. A moment later, the engine caught and *Honoured End* growled up the slope. Castigon opened the side hatch. Forcas brought the Rhino level with the captain. Corbulo grabbed Castigon by the shoulders and hauled him into the vehicle.

Castigon turned on him. His face was drenched in blood, some dripping from his fangs. He swung his chainsword. Corbulo ducked beneath the blow and rushed at Castigon. He rammed the captain against the side wall of the Rhino. He was fighting to subdue, but Castigon was fighting to kill. He had to break through Castigon's Thirst now or not at all. 'Forcas!' he called and brought the Red Grail up before the Lord Adjudicator's eyes.

The Rhino halted and Forcas entered the troop hold. He added his weight to keep Castigon pinned.

The howls of the rest of Fourth Company rocked the interior of *Honoured End*.

'The holy relic guided you back to us before, brother-captain,' Corbulo said. 'Remember it. The blood of our father was shed into this cup. It was shed for us. Turn from the blood of corruption. The blood of nobility calls to you, Castigon. It calls to the same nobility in you. Answer it. Follow it.'

Castigon struggled in their grip. He gnashed his teeth. In the red cast of his eyes, Corbulo saw none of the majesty he knew was there. The Castigon who had led the Knights of Baal for centuries had vanished, but he was one with his company. His men had followed him into the killing madness.

Corbulo called to him again. And again. He held the Red Grail up, and its light filled the hold. And still Castigon howled his desperate hunger for blood. Corbulo remembered Lemartes' dismissal of his attempts to help the Chaplain come out of the fugues of the Black Rage. Lemartes had returned to rationality with no help from him. What if his efforts were futile here too? If Castigon's earlier recovery had been due solely to his own will, then he had devoted himself to futility, and hope for the Chapter dimmed a little bit more.

He would not accept that.

'*Castigon*,' he commanded, '*Sanguinius recalls you to your duty!*'

Corbulo's sense of his physical being vanished. Castigon, too, ceased to be, as did Forcas and the compartment. The dread rain faded away. The mate-rium reduced itself to the Red Grail. It was the memory and spirit of the Blood Angels. It was the tangible sign of all that was great in their past. In this suspended moment, it was also the promise of their future. The promise that the Chapter *had* a future.

The world returned. Castigon gasped. He tried to raise his arms. He was no longer snarling. Corbulo nodded to Forcas and they stepped back, releasing Castigon. He reached for the Grail. Corbulo gave it to him. Castigon collapsed, clutching the chalice with both hands. His prayers were whispered, exhausted, rapid. When he stood, his eyes were clear, though shadowed. He reverently passed the Grail back to Corbulo.

Forcas slid the hatch closed, muffling the snarls and the butchery.

'What is happening to us?' Castigon said. The question did not need an answer. It was as close to an expression of despair as Corbulo had ever heard Castigon utter. 'Have we all succumbed?' the captain asked.

'All the battle-brothers caught in this rain have, yes,' Corbulo said.

Castigon winced. 'The pull is still strong.'

'The vehicles provide some shelter,' Corbulo told him. 'It is imperfect, but all we have.'

'And not enough shelter for the entire company.'

'No.' Not even close. Three Rhinos. Enough for the Death Company. Enough for a fraction of the Fourth. Rescued one at a time.

'What is the situation at the gates?'

'I saw something as we drew alongside you, captain,' Forcas began.

Honoured End shook, interrupting him. The shaking continued, growing worse. An earthquake.

'A daemon has been summoned,' Forcas said as they braced themselves.

'And Lemartes?'

'The Death Company is still in the fight.'

'We need them here,' Castigon said.

'You have a strategy in mind?' Corbulo asked.

'That will be up to the Chaplain to tell us,' Castigon said, his face a mixture of anguish and determination. He was a proud warrior. He was also the Lord Adjudicator. Corbulo had seen Castigon's fabled judgement at work often enough as he negotiated Chapter politics. Now it superseded his pride. The best way he could serve his stricken company was to accept that another was better suited to lead it though this crisis. 'Lemartes is the Guardian of the Lost,' Castigon said, 'and we are all lost now. He must lead Fourth Company into battle. He will be our salvation, Brother Corbulo.'

The ground heaved.

The rain, deluge and flood. The world turned into the fall and rush of blood. It fell on Reinecker. It was a spiritual corrosive. It came to wash away the last of hope, honour, duty, pride. The last of meaning. It would leave only anger. He was rooted to the spot.

He had been shooting the wrathful of Phlegethon, advancing towards the Blood Disciples, and then the blood had come, staggering him, banishing thought. He stood there, bolt pistol still extended, finger frozen, as the rage sought to take full possession of him.

He fought it. He rejected it. His voice hoarse, he called out to his regiment. 'Remember who you are! No passion can shake our discipline!'

Stromberg echoed him, and the shout was picked up by the other officers down the column. Reinecker took a step. The action was a blow against the anarchy that scrabbled at the doors of his mind. Another step. He was Mordian. He was the cold precision of war and faith. He marched forward, always forward. He did so now, and his regiment followed.

At his core, giving strength to the discipline, was a precious ember. His faith in the teachings of the Ecclesiarchy was destroyed. It was less than ash. But beneath that was the flame that nourished every other aspect of his being: his belief in the God-Emperor. Without that, there was nothing that could be said to *be* Iklaus Reinecker.

He prayed. He had no consciousness of the words, only of their intent, and of the rhythm of the prayer. It was the drumbeat of his march. He prayed with all the more fervour when the thing burst from the mound of rubble. The winged, horned, gigantic figure of myth battered the world with its roar. The daemon struck the ground with its axes. Around it, the Traitor Space Marines transformed into monstrosities. Some became things far more terrible and powerful than they had been before. What gods they worshipped had answered them.

The daemon raised its axes again, and Phlegethon began to tear itself open.

A god walked before Reinecker.

But he walked with his. 'The Emperor protects!' he shouted.

The cry was a desperate truth. It was also a command to the regiment.

'*The Emperor protects!*' came back from thousands of throats.

Even now, Reinecker thought. *Even here, in this terrible place, before this terrible foe, the Emperor protects, and I will fight for Him.*

The 237th Siege Regiment of the Mordian Iron Guard marched in perfect lockstep, weapons at the ready. Discipline marched to make a final stand against a rage to split worlds.

My brothers answer my call. I cannot say what forges my links with them. My words, my gestures, my presence, my will, my madness. Any of these. All of them. I do not need to understand. It is enough that I am one with the martyrs of the Death Company, and they with me. We gather for a concerted attack on Skarbrand.

We face the daemon that Commander Dante bested in single combat. Their struggle is legend. Now we must be worthy of the Chapter Master. I do not know if the daemon thinks. If he remembers the battle and seeks vengeance on the Chapter. Has his rage been growing since that defeat? The question is irrelevant. My task is the same.

The span of time is brief from the moment of the daemon's arrival to the moment of our readiness. Much happens in that span. Events and reason intervene before we launch.

The Blood Disciples transform. Their forms contort. Flesh and armour become monstrous. They become physical embodiments of rage. Where rage is uncontrolled, the forms are anarchic. They are an explosion of mindless aggression. But some in their number still retain some form of order. Their rage gives them strength, as I well know it can.

Skarbrand strikes the ground, and something of immense import begins to happen to Phlegethon. The wound in the earth spreads outward from his axes. It lengthens. The sides draw apart with the deep cracking of stone.

And the Iron Guard still marches forward. Still in formation. The Mordians begin to fire on Skarbrand. They cannot hope to survive this engagement. Yet they are a miracle. They still hold out against the contagion of rage.

I think again that they must be a source of hope. Their doomed charge must lead to something greater.

As the land convulses, Castigon calls to me on the vox. His voice cuts through the choir of snarls. He urges me to return to Fourth Company. 'You must lead us, Chaplain Lemartes,' he says.

The Lord Adjudicator is correct. But we need time, and Skarbrand will be on us in moments.

And then Reinecker performs his miracle.

The 237th closed in on the gates of Phlegethon, cutting through the surviving wrathful who still blocked the way. Reinecker fought to keep his feet as the ground bucked and the crevasse spread towards the Blood Angels. The Iron Guard were approaching the monstrous host from the flank. The huge daemon began to advance on the Space Marines. It and the transformed Blood Disciples paid no attention to the advance of the Mordians.

Reinecker saw opportunity.

'Pass the word,' he called. 'On my command, all fire at the daemon.'

He waited for the order to reach the rear of the column, still marching forward. He knew what would happen when he gave the signal. He and his troops were living the last moments of their lives. But this felt right. This felt like victory. The blood fell and fell and fell, and each drop ate at his will, sapping his ability to maintain discipline. Blind rage expanded in his chest. He would not be able to keep it at bay for much longer.

A little longer, though. Just a little. Enough.

The strength of the Blood Angels had been split. He would buy them time. If that made a difference, then that was a true victory.

He would die as a Mordian, and he would die for his Emperor.

He raised his pistol. They were within range. '*Fire!*' he ordered.

The volley came in a succession of close waves, the rear ranks shooting as soon as they saw the forward elements unleashing their lasweapons. Thousands of shots converged on the single target. They hit with enough force to knock the daemon off its stride.

I have your attention, Reinecker thought.

The daemon turned. It charged the Iron Guard, the Blood Disciples following in its wake. Its roar washed over the regiment. Reinecker's discipline and order crumbled, but still he held. 'Fire,' he gasped. He could barely hear his own voice. No matter. His last command still remained, and the Mordians fired again, and again, the volleys becoming even more synchronised. The daemon ran full-on into the blasts and did not slow. New earth tremors came with its every step. Reinecker stood his ground and fired his pistol. Terror and anger clawed at him. The blood was ankle-deep. But he held on.

They all did.

Then the daemon was upon them. Reinecker and Stromberg ducked beneath the first sweeps of the immense axes. So many others did not. The slaughter was huge. In a single blow, a hundred troopers died, their bodies flying in bloody chunks across the battlefield. The daemon waded into the regiment, cutting the Mordians down by scores with every movement. Reinecker found himself to one side of the horror, its shredded wings shadowing him from above. He fired up at the daemon's eyes. He hit. The daemon gazed down at him.

The terror brought him to his knees. But he fired one more time. And as the axe came for him, cutting Stromberg in half, pouring Mordian blood into the growing lake, Reinecker shouted his triumph at the daemon.

He had turned it from its path. He had resisted the plague of rage until the end.

Beneath the terror, entwined with faith, pride flared once more.

Reinecker knew the touch of redemption in the moment before the axe hit.

The Death Company launches away from Skarbrand. We put distance between ourselves and the daemons even as they turn their anger on the Mordians. Our flight looks like a retreat. It feels like one. Yet I maintain the unity of my squads. We race to the better weapon. I do not speak those words. Even so, I communicate this strategy to the Death Company. What do we see?

Daemons on Terra.

We see the obscene. The impossible. That which must not be suffered to exist.

The worst of Traitors. The worst of betrayals. The war growing desperate.

Urgency. As if we might save the Angel.

Save him. Avenge him. Contradictory beliefs. We hold them both. I alone have the knowledge, for now, of the delusion. I share the belief of my brothers and I know it is mad. I am divided against myself.

I pray this schism will save us all.

Fourth Company's position is a single jump away. We come down as the daemon responds to the provocation of the Iron Guard with a vast slaughter. The Blood Disciples, in worship, do not leave his side. The Mordians keep fighting. They have won us valuable seconds. Time to forge the counter-attack. We will make the mortals' sacrifice count.

We land on violent ground. The tremors are growing worse, and more widespread. Crevasses open, multiply, deepen.

There is a pattern to the destruction. Its revelation will not be welcome.

Fourth Company is in the grip of the Thirst. Its battle-brothers are unleashed. They butcher whatever human comes within their grasp. This is not a fighting force. It is a riot. It is debased. Animals in ceramite pour more blood into the deepening lake of vitae that covers the plain.

Everything is collapsing. The land. The Blood Angels. I am the rational one amid a sea of insanity. The situation is desperate.

Castigon calls from *Honoured End*. 'Chaplain Lemartes,' he says, 'will you lead us?'

'I will.'

'There is little the rest of us can do. The tanks can provide support for now. As to the rest...'

'I know what I must do.'

'I pray that you do. We have no other options.'

'You do not,' I agree.

I have no more choice than he does.

To the east, the Iron Guard are finished. Skarbrand approaches. There is no more time.

Fourth Company and the Death Company. The two curses have swallowed the campaign. Their differences are great. The Black Rage is the distortion of thought and honour. The Red Thirst is the absence of all thought.

But they both end in blood. They are both enacted fury.

I plunge deeper into the grip of the Rage. The past becomes reality, and with it comes the fury at loss and great betrayal. But as I fall, I hold tight to the knowledge of *now* and *here*. But I sink, and I sink, and I sink. Divided, split, I resist and I succumb, rational and raving. I am paradox.

My strand of reason is thin. It must be adamantium.

My soul, my mind, my heart, my arms. They are suffused with wrath. Vengeance that has waited ten thousand years teaches me all the shades of rage. I know it all. I understand it all. Even the Thirst. That degradation is in our core, like the other curse.

I draw a breath. Through my rebreather, I taste the blood in the air. I fill my lungs. And then I roar.

A roar for justice. For the ten thousand years. For the destruction of the enemy. For the blood.

For the tragedy of the Blood Angels.

The Death Company hears. Fourth Company hears. We are joined in the most primal, murderous fashion.

And so I command.

The enemy approaches. My roar is answered by Skarbrand. The daemon's bellow is deafening. It splits stone with its power. I cannot match its brute force. But it is without thought. It is inchoate anger.

I still hold on to the *here*, the *now*. This is Phlegethon. I am Lemartes.

I lead my army to war.

Corbulo looked through a forward viewing block of *Honoured End*. His sense of the battlefield was limited. The Rhino jerked up and down with the movements of the earth, blurring the perspective. The Sanguinary High Priest could only see a narrow slice of the terrain ahead. He longed to be on the storm bolter's turret, but while the rain of blood continued, neither he nor Castigon could emerge from the shelter of the vehicle. They were reduced to being observers. As frustrated as he was, at least he wasn't in Castigon's position. In effect, the captain had been forced to relinquish command. The distinction between Fourth Company and the savage population of Phlegethon had blurred. The guardian of the Death Company now had control. The mad leading the mad.

Forcas was just as frustrated by the enforced inaction. 'There must be something we can do,' the driver said.

'We have mass,' Castigon said.

Corbulo nodded. He watched the daemonic host

close with their position. He saw Fourth Company sweep forward in fury behind Lemartes. He noted the size and shape of some of the enemy. 'Agreed,' he said. 'This vehicle is our weapon.'

'Tanks, open fire,' Castigon ordered on the company vox-channel. 'Rhinos, charge the foe.'

Honoured End lurched forward. The ground dropped suddenly on the right, and they almost flipped over. Forcas managed to steer onto more level terrain and increased his speed. Corbulo stayed at his post, watching, bearing witness. The sheets of descending blood, the advance of Skarbrand, the attack of the frenzied Blood Angels. *Mark this,* he thought. *Mark all of this. Learn from this day if another dawn breaks. Stand with your brothers if it does not.*

'What will be left of us?' Castigon asked. He spoke as quietly as the growl of the engine and the hammering of the earthquakes allowed.

'Enough,' Corbulo said. 'There will be enough.' He would not believe otherwise. He could not afford to do so. But the shadows of visions that haunted his rest drew closer, gathering definition.

He gazed upon a full company consumed by madness, and the shadow of the future took form.

The land is in agony. It screams. The convulsions increase in intensity. Waves of rock rise and fall. Behind Fourth Company, the crevasses widen and deepen, become gorges, become canyons. The battlefield launches twisted columns upwards. It sinks and rises with the crack and thunder of splintering rock and straining magma. Explosions chew up the ground. The Predators are firing their guns. Accuracy is impossible, but one of the mutated Blood Disciples goes down, blown apart by assault cannon fire. We of the Death Company shoot forward with our jump packs. We leave the flowing ground behind. Now there is only our attack.

The Blood Disciples are just ahead of Skarbrand. The daemon's strides are deliberate. He stops with each to reap a harvest of blood from the mortals around him. He cuts a dozen down with an axe, while gathering up a handful of squirming victims. He devours their skulls, then hurls the twitching, fountaining bodies ahead of him. Some of his victims are Iron Guard. A few still remain, fighting to the last.

We clash with the Blood Disciples. Many of them still have jump packs, even when they are part of their new bodies. Others, who did not fly before, have wings now. The Traitor Chaplain who fought me on the Prophet's hill is one of those. His robe now has veins and structure. It flaps, and he rises to intercept me. I change the angle of my flight. I hit him hard. We crash to the ground. He is one of the least transformed, though his hands have become giant pincers. They wrap around my head as we grapple. He would crush my skull. I cannot see. He snarls a gospel of obscenity. I roar my litany of rage back at him and swing the Blood Crozius. My blow crushes

his left arm. The pincer drops. I can see through my
right lens. The Crozius flares, its essence outraged
by the presence of daemonic flesh. It is hungry for
more retribution. So am I.

I fire my jump pack, and carry us both upwards.
The Traitor's wings beat the air and me. His remaining pincer holds fast, squeezes harder, though my
helmet resists. Eldritch light arcs between his multi-
foliate horns. I raise my bolt pistol to his face. The
light strikes me. The assault is psychic. My armour is
no defence. My mind's eye sees nothing but blood.
Boiling, corrupted blood. The deluge of the Traitor's
rage. It is a blow that would kill a mortal. It could cast
a fellow Adeptus Astartes into madness.

It runs up against my own rage. It collides with
righteousness.

I am not Mephiston. My counter is not psychic. But
it serves me well. The Crozius blazes with the purity
of extermination. I bring it down on the Traitor's
skull. I bisect him down to the chest. The two halves
of his head shriek as we fall back to the ground. Tentacles reach out between the hemispheres. They try
to make him whole again. But his mind is divided.
His anger becomes diffuse. He is dying. His body
loses coherence. Before we touch the ground, it is at
war with itself, mutating uncontrollably.

The battle is an explosion of anger. There is no
strategy. I direct the larger movements of Fourth
Company, but all other forms of military structure
have collapsed. Assault, tactical and devastator

squads are intermixed. I designate the enemy, and my frenzied brothers hurl themselves into the cauldron. They attack with chainsword and lightning claws and power fist. Their fury cannot tolerate the cold distance of bolter fire. They must smash the blood from the enemy. The Blood Disciples oblige. Monsters clash with berserkers under a drowning fall of blood. As if further enraged by the conflict, the land responds with ever greater violence. Pits open and slam shut. They are snapping jaws of stone. The columns rise only to topple. They are limbs. Clubs. Weapons.

The planet has joined the war on the side of the enemy. The wrath that has shaped it is the wrath of the dark god whose servants we fight. It negates our advantage of numbers. Its jaws and limbs target the Blood Angels. Brother Phenex is trapped by closing stone, his legs crushing to nothing. He fights still, grasping for the nearest enemy. The Traitor with an arm that has become a chainaxe steps behind and decapitates him. Sergeant Gamigin is almost flattened when rock reaches out and falls. He survives through chance and the speed of his pursuit of a kill. He never realises his danger. He, like all his afflicted brothers, has little awareness of his surroundings. He responds only to the Thirst and to the immediate presence of a threat.

The Death Company compensates for the ground's assault. The Black Rage changes our reality. It translates what we see into something else, but we still see it. The madness of reality is nothing to those whose perception is already distortion.

A Rhino, *Blood Requiem*, passes me at full speed. The wrathful disappear under its treads. It bucks over the rippling ground. A column of rock bursts upward just past its rear. A second earlier and it would have overturned the vehicle. *Blood Requiem* drives through the struggling remains of the mob and makes directly for one of the contorted Blood Disciples. The Traitor no longer has features. He is a crawling mass as high as the Rhino. *Blood Requiem* smashes into him. Blood splashes. The Traitor is not dead. He has absorbed much of the shock. *Blood Requiem*'s treads spray blood and viscera as they seek traction. The mutation writhes and flails against the hull. He cannot pierce the armour. He holds the vehicle in place as he is gradually pulled under and shredded. Skarbrand closes in.

I launch. I streak towards the daemon. Something explodes against my flank. I am out of control. I slam into the ground. My armour smokes from the auto-cannon shell. Damage runes cascade across my lenses. Pain is a grasping, electric hand. It will not slow me down. It fans the flames of rage.

I am on my feet and charging. I am too late. Skarbrand looms over the Rhino. He smashes his axes down. The blows split the armour open like an eggshell. Warp light flows from them into the vehicle. It spreads like an infection over the hull. The metal bends. Keeping *Blood Requiem* pinned with one blade, the daemon strikes again with the other. The warpglow blossoms. The Rhino implodes, its sides crumpling as if clenched by an invisible fist. There is a pulse. And then an explosion. *Blood Requiem* and its occupants disintegrate. They fly across the field in fragments, trailing the foul light.

'*For the Emperor!*' I yell. The battle cry of the Blood Angels is meaningless to Fourth Company. It means everything to the Death Company. '*For Sanguinius!*' It has not changed since the days of the Heresy. It is there in our blood. In our pride. In our Flaw. '*Death! Death!*'

The word is our meaning and our identity.

Comet streaks of the Death Company closing with me on Skarbrand. Our brothers swarm the Blood Disciples. The explosion of the Rhino has created a space, a clear shot at the daemon. We fire on approach. The shells bounce off the monster's hide. It turns to meet us and roars. Three of my brothers are in the direct blast of that sound. The air itself writhes in the cone of the roar. The sound is a missile of rage. When it hits my brothers, their wrath becomes warp energy and they explode. They fall to the ground, broken corpses engulfed in psychic flames. The rest of us are outside the cone, but the effects of the daemonic rage still reach us. Reality becomes even more fluid.

A ghost image is summoned by my curse. The Imperial Palace.

No.

I clamp down hard on the real. I have lost only a fraction of a second of time. My flight is still true. Skarbrand draws another breath. His eyes are blank, without thought. Yet I read desperation in them.

What makes a daemon desperate? Not us.

The reflection is a flash of unfinished thought. Before Skarbrand roars again, we are upon him. I strike his chest with the Blood Crozius. Where bolter shells failed, the sacred relic draws the daemon's blood. My surviving brothers are right behind me. They surround the daemon and assail him with blows as righteous as they are maddened.

It is not enough.

Skarbrand smashes me aside with the flat of a blade. He hurls me to the ground hard enough to plough a furrow in the unstable rock. On the instant, I am attacked by the wrathful. They are a flood of doomed vermin. I shake them off as I rise.

Skarbrand whirls, striking at my brothers, hurling them aside. I lose two more when he cuts them in half, bringing axe blades together in a cross stroke. The daemon roars at the sky, quivering with anger.

He spreads his ruined wings. He beats at the air. He rises, the movement ponderous at first. The wings are so damaged they should not work at all. Still he climbs. Then, ten metres off the ground, he pauses. His arms are outstretched, his jaws gape wide. The air around him shimmers as reality is stretched to the breaking point. Recovered, I start my jump. I must stop what is coming. My brothers are with me.

We are too late. Skarbrand roars again, and from the span of his wings comes a great crimson fire. It spreads wider as it streams from him. It envelops us all. It is burning blood. Blinded, coated with the flaming vitae, I drop to the ground again. I wipe the flames from my helmet, but all I can see is the fire. Its propagation is a storm. All the blood, on the ground and in the air, combusts.

The battlefield is consumed by burning wrath.

CHAPTER TEN

Inferno

Corbulo and Castigon watched though the forward viewing blocks of *Honoured End* as the burning blood washed over the land. Blood Angels and Blood Disciples became struggling torches. The mortals came to their final end. The pyres of the individual deaths were swallowed in the enormous conflagration. Visibility was subject to the currents of flood and fire. One moment Corbulo could see where the raging Skarbrand flew and the Death Company struggled forward, and in the next he could see nothing but waves of crimson flame. He saw fragments of the war: the corpses of mortals who drowned as they burned, the clash of maddened Blood Angels against the mutated foe.

He saw battle-brothers fall.

Forcas hit a serpentine Traitor with the Rhino. He

backed up, then ran over the daemonic foe again, grinding the body to pulp. Then he slowed the vehicle to a crawl. Between the firestorm and the heaving earth, every metre forward risked destruction.

'We cannot stay in here.' Castigon spoke with shame and anger.

'We have no choice, Lord Adjudicator.'

'We are abandoning our brothers.'

'They are not abandoned. They are led by Lemartes. As you commanded.'

Castigon said nothing. Corbulo felt the same frustration. But to hurl themselves out and fall to Thirst and flame would be an abdication of duty.

There was a heavy thump on the roof of the Rhino. Then an impossible sound: flesh grinding through metal. A rent appeared through the upper hatch. Sparks and drops of flame scattered into the compartment. As the shielding tore, Corbulo felt the spiritual poison of the blood reach inside. Castigon's breathing became strained, almost a growl. The stench of blood tore again at Corbulo's self-control. He held fast and took a position three steps forward of the hatch, Heaven's Teeth in his right hand, the Red Grail in his left.

A flesh-covered chainaxe cut all the way through the hatch. It withdrew. Heavy blows smashed the two halves of the door in. It fell to the vehicle's deck. The burning rain and a Blood Disciple followed. The Traitor's arm and chainaxe had become one. His reach was huge. He brought the weapon down in a vertical slash. Corbulo blocked it with Heaven's Teeth. Relic and daemonic transformation fought. The Rhino filled with a sound that was roar of bone and scream of metal. Blood from the Traitor and flames from the sky splattered over Corbulo. The Thirst sank its claws into his throat and mind. The world became fevered. He clutched the Grail harder. He concentrated on its reality, on its strength.

The Blood Disciple leaned in to the attack. He had grown in his mutation, bursting through his armour. His mass was easily half again Corbulo's. The chain-axe pushed down. The whirring blades approached Corbulo's face.

Castigon fired his bolt pistol. The shells slammed into the Traitor's shoulder. Blood gouted, but the hulking Space Marine didn't react. Light, the violet of rotting meat, crackled around his blade. It touched Heaven's Teeth, and set off a flash of warring energies. The Thirst urged Corbulo to surrender discipline, to launch himself at the Blood Disciple and tear the Traitor's throat out with his teeth.

He knew he would die if he gave in to his instinct.

He held the Grail in his hand and in his mind. He felt its purity. He pulled it into his bloodstream. Its light cleansed the corruption. Its strength united with the brutal nobility of Heaven's Teeth.

The light from the Grail washed back over the Traitor. Heaven's Teeth cut through the chainaxe blade. Vitae and bone chips flew in a storm. The Traitor howled and staggered back, his stump of an arm-weapon flooding his life onto the Rhino's deck. Corbulo drove Heaven's Teeth forward, through the Blood Disciple's helmet and skull. The enemy dropped like a felled grox.

Corbulo turned back to Castigon. The captain leaned against the bulkhead, bolt pistol still out, teeth bared, breathing laboured.

'Captain?' Corbulo said.

'I... I am with you still,' Castigon gasped.

Corbulo took a step towards him. There was the sudden impact of stone against metal. The ground heaved upwards, and the Rhino was rolling. Corbulo held on to the relics as he was tossed from wall to wall. When *Honoured End* came to a stop, it was on its side.

Castigon pushed himself to his feet. He staggered over to Corbulo and grabbed his arm. 'We must go out there,' he said. 'Lemartes leads us in the darkness, Brother Corbulo. You must give us the light.' His breath was laboured, but his eyes were still clear. They were fixed on the aura of the Red Grail.

Corbulo nodded. Holding the Grail before him, he stepped into the storm of flame.

Over the hiss and hollow wind of the flaming blood, I hear a paroxysm of snarls on the vox. The inferno drives Fourth Company towards a terminal frenzy. The Blood Angels are animals, goaded by the Thirst and the fire. My armour withstands the flame for the moment, but the temperature is rising, and the burning rivulets seek my flesh through seams and cracks. There are brothers on the ground whose armour has taken worse blows, others with no helmets. We are losing many.

Still I call to them. Still I reach out in madness and rage and urge Fourth Company forward. The enemy obliges with his presence. The Blood Angels recognise the Blood Disciples as foes, even if nothing else in the way of thought remains. The war continues. I can hear it on the channels. I hear the rending of flesh. There is even some bolter fire. I am surprised. I am further surprised when I glimpse a piercing, stable glow amidst the flame. There is purity in that light. There is strength. That is the light of untainted blood.

Corbulo, I think.

A glimmer of hope, and yet we are blind. Reality has disappeared behind a shifting wall of crimson flame. We are being immolated in a reality given over to a god of blood and fire.

One reality. There is another...

Even as the thought occurs to me, a monster lands before me. His armour and flesh are one, and on the embedded plates I can see the traces of a captain's insignia. And so I know from our records who this being was! Khevrak. He strikes with his claws. They cut through my armour on both flanks, slicing deep into my flesh, breaking ribs. He snaps his massive jaws down. I twist, and they do not close over my head. Teeth centimetres long bite into my right

pauldron. Daemon-forged, they are strong enough
to puncture the ceramite. For a moment they are
stuck. I propel myself forward. The ramming force
is almost enough to break Khevrak's neck. He yanks
his jaws free and stumbles back. I swing the Crozius,
and it smashes open his upper chest. The wound is a
canyon. Blood flashes into steam. His howl is one of
disbelief. He lashes out with his claws again, and they
sink deeper this time. But I have struck once more
too, burying the Crozius in the injury. We are locked
together for several seconds, each tearing open our
enemy's wounds.

'You will not find redemption here, either,' Khevrak
snarls at me. My bones on both sides begin to grate.
Something jabs a lung.

'I do not seek it,' I tell him and force the Crozius
through his breastplate. I destroy what lies beneath.

Khevrak goes limp. His arms fall to his side. He
collapses.

I find his last words to me curious. Why speak of
redemption? Why would Traitors seek it?

And what makes a daemon desperate?

I am aware of confused fighting around me. One
of my brothers in the Death Company falls from the
sky. He lands twice. He has been cut in half vertically.

We need unity again. We need to see again.

The blood burned. The trails of new scars opened
on Corbulo's face. The flames billowed around him.
They dripped from his arms. But he was a Space

Marine, and pain was irrelevant. What mattered was that the fire could not pull him into the Red Thirst. As he walked with the Grail held high, it shone with all the force of his faith concentrated and reflected by the sacred blood it had once held. Beside him Castigon marched, and he too resisted. He opened fire with his bolter on a Blood Disciple who approached. Recoiling from the light of the Grail, the monster's defences dropped, and Castigon's shells blew off his head.

They passed Gamigin, and though the sergeant's frenzy did not abate, when the Grail drew near, he leapt on his opponent with greater strength. His gauntlets plunged into the Blood Disciple's serpentine neck and tore it wide open.

'No redemption,' Castigon croaked.

'Not without time,' said Corbulo. But perhaps Castigon was wrong. The touch of purity added force to the brothers who felt it. Even with the fire, and the twisting of the land, the tide began to turn against the Blood Disciples.

He wanted to see hope in this. He knew he could not as long as Skarbrand walked the battlefield.

I cannot find Skarbrand in the flames. I gather the Death Company, its numbers reduced further with every moment as the daemon finds my brothers and cuts them down. They fall from all sides. He must be circling the field. I cannot orient myself in the vortices of flaming blood. The blood swirls around us, falling from the heavens, rising at our feet. The burn flows down me, obscuring my vision, distracting with mounting damage. In the end, this rain will eat us to nothing.

We are blind in this reality. So I must turn to the other.

The strain is great. The risk greater still. I loosen my grip on the real. I let the past take over. As I do, I know that overturning the balance might mean I will be lost in the delusion of the Black Rage forever.

I fall into the vision. The burning blood fades. The world reshapes itself into the halls of a battle-barge. We seek the great enemy, and it is only here that we will find him. Walls of stone and blasphemous iconography rise above me. I see the enemy. I see Horus.

I am wracked by burning pain. There is why: Horus has slain the Angel. 'Brothers!' I cry. 'Avenge our father!'

As one, we streak towards Horus.

The weakened portion of my mind that knows this is delusion cries out to me. I have found the enemy, but I cannot fight him through a lie.

The wrench is massive. I am torn between two times, two worlds, two reals. But I see the truth again. I lead the Death Company in a direct flight through the billowing fire of blood at Skarbrand. All our force is concentrated into a spear formation. We unleash a hail of bolter fire before us.

Skarbrand flinches. The shells damage his form.

The answer comes to me. Why would Traitors seek redemption? What makes a daemon desperate?

Betrayal.

Somehow, in some form, Skarbrand and the Blood Disciples are wracked with regret for a betrayal. I do not have to know its nature. It is enough to know the weakness is there. And in this moment, the warriors of the Death Company believe themselves to be avenging the greatest betrayal in our history.

Our shells are striking Skarbrand with the force of justice. Justice for betrayal. We strike at the daemon's weakness: his consciousness of sin.

He retaliates with still greater fury. The axes come together with blood and fire and the searing, jagged black of rage. I see the blow coming. I kill the propulsion of my jump pack and drop down. My brothers see an attack, but they see Horus, and Skarbrand is a colossus. The lie of the vision dooms many. The materium screams as the axes collide. Figures in black armour are torn apart by the fragmenting real.

But there are still more of us, and the charge continues. Skarbrand roars in pain and wrath. He smashes more of the Death Company to the ground at the same time that I am rising again. I shoot up, straight up, between the massive sweeps of the daemon's weapons. At the zenith of my climb, I am level with his eyes. I bring the Blood Crozius down with all the strength of purified, holy wrath upon his skull. The sacred relic shatters bone.

Skarbrand's roar deafens me. He drops an axe and

snatches me out of the air. His grip is crushing. I cannot breathe. I feel my frame splinter. But my arms are free and I strike again.

Focused on me, he has left himself open to the rest of the Death Company. The shells from my brothers hit his chest and throat at same time. Daemonic ichor sprays into the air, combusting when it contacts the flaming blood.

Still holding me, Skarbrand looks down. His lethal roar falls upon my brothers.

But they have fired one last volley.

And I strike one more time.

And the sin of the daemon overwhelms his material form. With a howl to blot out all light, he loses the coherence of his rage. He explodes. And all realities disappear in the instant of absolute conflagration.

EPILOGUE

Undertow

The light of wrath fades. I am lying on the ground. My breathing sounds like stones dragged over iron. Fragments of bone tear at my lungs. One of my hearts has stopped. My Larraman's organ labours to staunch my wounds. I teeter on the edge of sus-an membrane coma.

Where am I?

I force myself to rise to my knees. A full minute later, I finally stand. I look around. I am on Terra. Is the battle over? All is silence. Is the Palace saved?

The uncertainty shakes me. There is no such uncertainty in the past.

No.

Not Terra.

My hold on the present, as tenuous as my consciousness, forces me to look again. Reality reassembles itself.

I see the landscape of Phlegethon. But it feels insubstantial. Distant. The immediacy of the past pulls at me. The Rage is there, but not aftermath. The tug is strong.

I stagger forward, leaning against the wind of my curse. I look around, forcing myself to absorb details, fighting to create a reality with some weight. The landscape is littered with corpses half-submerged in an endless mire of blood. A fetid mist rolls over the terrain, mixing with smoke laden with the stench of burned flesh. The deluge is over, though. The fire is out. The land is still. The psychic rage that fuelled them all has been banished.

I walk through the fog and tally the cost. The Death Company, Fourth Company, Iron Guard, Blood Disciples. The murdered population of Phlegethon. So many bodies. Too many brothers and allies. Many enemies, but not quite enough. The Blood Disciples have left the field, but I do not think we killed them all. I thought I had finished Khevrak, but I do not see him here.

One tally is complete. My battle-brothers of the Death Company have found peace. Their deaths were violent, killed by Skarbrand or by his immolation. But they are free now of the endless wrath and grief.

As I move away from the epicentre of Skarbrand's fall, I find the living. Fourth Company exists once more. The Red Thirst has left most of the Blood Angels. They have been able to contain our brothers who did not recover when the rain and its toxic power ended.

At a cost.

We have inflicted more losses on ourselves.

I find Corbulo outside *Honoured End.*

'I rejoice to see you, Chaplain Lemartes,' he says.

'And I you.' A partial lie. Rejoicing is a lost country to me. But Corbulo's survival is an unalloyed good. 'Captain Castigon...?'

Corbulo smiles. 'He is well. With my help he fought the Red Thirst. He is with the wounded.' He gestures to a tent set up a few dozen metres away. 'And you, Chaplain. You are injured, but...'

'Do not ask me what I see, Brother Corbulo. I am still mistrustful of my eyes. The pull grows stronger.' I descended too far in the Black Rage. The strain to remain afloat in the ocean is greater than it has ever been. My wounds are extensive, but they are trivial. The waves of the ocean are high, and there is a great undertow. The day will come when I shall not surface.

'We will continue our work,' Corbulo says.

'No, brother.'

'Do not give up hope,' he protests.

'It is not a question of hope. It is a matter of acceptance, and of faith.'

'I don't understand.'

'The Rage defeated the daemon. My curse is my gift, Brother Corbulo. It is how I am meant to serve.'

I can see that he wishes to argue. My declaration is another loss. But he nods.

I step past him and open the rear hatch. I stand in

the Rhino and listen to the silence. No howls bounce off the interior of the hull. I am alone. The only cries I shall hear on the return journey are from the ghosts in my head. The ghosts who are becoming more real, and more present. I take the first seat. I look at Corbulo, who waits at the entrance. 'It is time,' I tell him. I was unleashed. We have won.

It is time to return to my chains.

ABOUT THE AUTHOR

David Annandale is the author of the
Horus Heresy novel *The Damnation of
Pythos* and the Primarchs novel *Roboute
Guilliman: Lord of Ultramar*. He has also
written *Warlord: Fury of the God-Machine*,
the Yarrick series, several stories involving
the Grey Knights, including *Warden of
the Blade*, and *The Last Wall, The Hunt
for Vulkan* and *Watchers in Death* for The
Beast Arises. For Space Marine Battles
he has written *The Death of Antagonis*
and *Overfiend*. He is a prolific writer of
short fiction set in The Horus Heresy,
Warhammer 40,000 and Age of Sigmar
universes. David lectures at a Canadian
university, on subjects ranging from English
literature to horror films and video games.

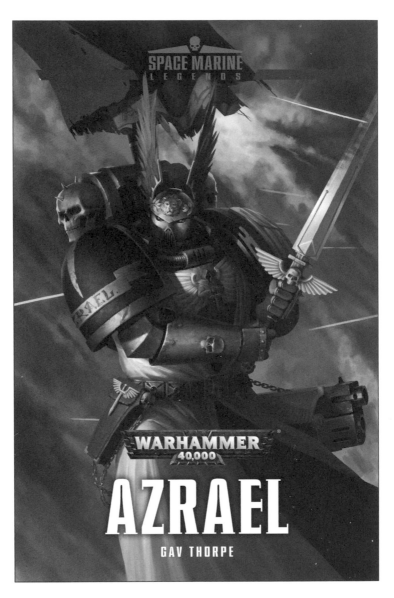

SPACE MARINE
LEGENDS

WARHAMMER
40,000

AZRAEL

GAV THORPE